HOUSE OF VAMPIRES

THE LORENA QUINN TRILOGY

SAMANTHA SNOW

Copyright ©2017 by Samantha Snow
All rights reserved.

Get Yourself a FREE Bestselling Paranormal Romance Book!

Join the "**Simply Shifters**" Mailing list today and gain access to an exclusive **FREE** classic Paranormal Shifter Romance book by one of our bestselling authors along with many others more to come. You will also be kept up to date on the best book deals in the future on the hottest new Paranormal Romances. We are the HOME of Paranormal Romance after all!

* Get FREE Shifter Romance Books For Your Kindle & Other Cool giveaways

* Discover Exclusive Deals & Discounts Before Anyone Else!

* Be The FIRST To Know about Hot New Releases From Your Favorite Authors

Click The Link Below To Access Get All This Now!

SimplyShifters.com

Already subscribed?
OK, *Turn The Page!*

About This Book

When Lorena Quinn went to live in the house of vampires she really did not know what to expect. With 4 vampires fighting for her love she knew that it was not always going to be easy.

And things took an interesting twist when Wei made a move on Lorena which caused Dmitri to fly into a jealous rage.

A rage so intense that it left Lorena wondering if she really had to fulfill the prophecy in this way, or perhaps there was another way out....

CHAPTER ONE
CHAPTER TWO
CHAPTER THREE
CHAPTER FOUR
CHAPTER FIVE
CHAPTER SIX
CHAPTER SEVEN
CHAPTER EIGHT
CHAPTER NINE
CHAPTER TEN
CHAPTER ELEVEN
CHAPTER TWELVE
CHAPTER THIRTEEN
CHAPTER FOURTEEN

CHAPTER ONE

What really sucked was that I knew it was a dream, but I still couldn't wake up. Most dreams were a foggy haze where things didn't fit together, like puzzle pieces from different boxes. This dream was real, too real, a half-remembered memory just distorted enough to know that I wasn't actually awake. It was full surround sound with the volume turned up and high definition television. It was full on 3D interactive with those fancy glasses and bright colors, a video game that I wanted to get lost in or maybe couldn't escape from.

In my too-real dream, I was sitting in the passenger's seat of an SUV. It, the car, not the seat, was too long to be realistic. There were an extra two bench seats so that it looked more like one of those weird stretch limos rather than the car that I remembered. The seats were filled with four vampire brothers, also known in the secret world of the paranormal as the Sons of Vlad. Yeah, that Vlad. Vlad the third, the second son of Vlad Dracula, more commonly known as The Impaler, and the very first vampire to ever walk the earth. There were three witches: one who I could only call organic, the other was very...mathematical, and then there was me, who was lucky enough to call myself a witch, if only just barely.

In the very back seat was Alan, who was quite possibly the most beautiful man who had ever been born. His angelic face was fixed into a charming and polite smile. His long golden hair floated around his angular face like a summer cloud. He wore dark leather pants on long slender legs and a sapphire blue French Renaissance jacket left unlaced to show off a bare chest. There were other men, bigger men, who were chiseled with washboard abs and other features. Not Alan. He was all slender lines and elegant beauty. His lips were parted just enough that I could see a glitter of fang.

"You'll have to choose, you know." He spoke French, but I knew what he said. I had never taken French. My years had been spent sitting in Mr. Bergen's German classes instead. Woe is me.

"Choose," he repeated.

Choosing. That's what this was all about. The reason why I was living in a great big mansion in the mountains of rural Virginia. The reason why I was learning about my history and the magic that lived inside of me. It was me deciding on one of three, or was that four now, who would become my beau and, ultimately, the father of a child of prophecy.

"I know," I said. My voice echoed strangely in my ears, like I was talking down a wind tunnel.

"How beautiful."

I was about to ask him what was beautiful when I realized his attention wasn't on me anymore; it was on the guy a few seats up.

The car rocked, shivering beneath me. I felt a trill of fear as we took a sharp turn around the mountain. I was pretty sure one of the wheels left the road, but no one else seemed bothered by it. Just me.

Dmitri, in his full Romani glory, was looking at me, completely unaware of Alan's provocative attention. He was dressed in black, but the outfit was out of date: loose billowing slacks trimmed with dark fur and a long vest so dark in hue that it got lost against the romantic profusion of curls. Beneath the vest, he wore a laced-up tunic left open just enough to catch a hint of the impressive musculature beneath. But I couldn't enjoy the view because of the look he was giving me. It wasn't a deep look, like you might give someone who was interesting to you, or even the soft look that happened when that special someone stepped into your view. It wasn't as if he cared that I was there, but that anyone was there, someone to give his intense attentions to.

"Pay attention to me," he said.

"I do," I promised.

The car shivered again, as if it knew something I didn't.

Then there was Zane, little more than a shadow, and not just because of the rich deep brown of his skin. His features were less perfect, less visceral from everyone else's. Perhaps because I didn't know him, perhaps because I knew he had been drained nearly to the point of death. I didn't know.

"You saved me." His voice made goosebumps appear on my unconscious flesh. It was deep and rich and precise, as if he thought about each and every word before it left his lips. "I will save you before the end."

The end of what? I wanted to ask him. The end of this prophecy? The end of this weird road trip? My whole life was a series of endings and beginnings. I needed him to be a little more precise.

The sky turned dark, and storm clouds in shades of purple, black, and green filled the horizon. It looked like rain but not the kind I'd wanna go out in.

"I don't know you," I whispered. I wasn't sure if I was talking to Zane or the impending storm. Maybe it was both.

What I did know was that the girl sitting next to him was the closest thing I had to a friend. Jenny sat with one of her long, athletic legs tucked up beneath the perfect point of her chin. Her skin, a deep burnished brown, shimmered with the bronze blush she liked to wear. She was reaching a hand cluttered with rings out to me, offering something that I couldn't actually see.

"Are you okay?" Jenny asked, her voice echoing similarly to my own.

Was I? Maybe. I didn't know that either. The dream was beginning to stretch, like too little fabric across too much skin. I didn't answer her, not because I didn't want to, but because my lips wouldn't move. I wanted to wake up, but the dream held me down.

"Are you okay?" she asked again.

When I could focus on her, the beautiful skin that she took such care of was cracking. A soft glow was spilling through the lines in her flesh.

"Are you?" I asked.

"I... don't know."

Count on Jenny to be the only one to answer me, even in a dream.

On the other side of her was another woman whose face was vivid, but the rest of her wasn't. She was hidden in a robe in shades of smoke. The center of her forehead held a diamond, like a bindi charm, which suited her, considering it was Reika. The apples of her cheeks were decorated with mathematics symbols. Not plus signs or anything like that, but strangely perfect interconnecting lines that formed pictures.

"Do you have to follow the prophecy?" she asked, her eyes flashing with a power I didn't really understand. "Do you have to end the world?"

Rain hit the windshield, green and acidic. Thunder, like the howling of wolves, rolled down the mountains. Everything started to shake. Fear turned inside of my belly. I didn't want to end the world.

"Ya gotta choose."

This voice, rich with the drawl of Appalachia, drew me to a woman I was sure hadn't been in the car before. Marquessa sat in the very back, next to Alan, and smiled an enigmatic smile that turned the deep mahogany of her cheeks into apples.

"No, she doesn't." a woman answered. I couldn't see her, but I knew my mother's voice now. "She can just walk away."

They started to bicker, but not with words. I knew they were arguing in the way that you simply know things in a dream, with unconscious certainty.

A hand reached out and touched my face. It was strong and sure. My fear dwindled inside of my belly, and I looked into eyes of flecked obsidian. Wei was beautiful in the way a sword was beautiful, honed to perfection. His long dark hair was coiled into a topknot, held in place by a bright band. A changsun top in shades of green brought out the natural gold in his skin. But he, more than anyone I had ever known, was more than a collection of colors and shapes. He was lethal and glorious and proud, and every emotion was held behind a perfect veneer, invisible unless you knew how to look. I knew, or I liked to think I did. He loved me; I could see it in those eyes.

"Watch me," he said, even as the SUV plummeted over the side of the mountain. I felt my stomach jump into my throat as we fell, and a dozen hands reached out to grab me as the rest of us fell. "Just watch."

I jerked awake with a suddenness that left me breathless. Rain pounded down against the window of my bedroom, turning the rose-stained glass into a pattern of colors through water. Lightening flickered in the distance, illuminating the shape of a man who stood in my bedroom doorway. I knew the shape instantly.

"Wei?" I asked, just in case I was still dreaming. A flash of lightning illuminated my otherwise dark bedroom. The usually warm wood of my furniture looked cold in the hard temporary brilliance.

"You cried out."

He was careful to keep his voice empty, but I knew better. I could feel him. I was...aware of him. To be fair, I was aware of the undead in general. I was a necromancer, or at least, that was what everyone was telling me; it gave me an edge when dealing with the undead. What all those edges were, I wasn't sure.

"Sorry," I said. I meant it. He looked tired. It was little more than a tightness around his eyes, but it was there. Everyone was tired. Not two days ago, we had escaped a compound of creepy cultists who thought that I shouldn't fulfill a prophecy. For some of us, the escape had been a near thing. A prophecy, by the way, that I had mixed feelings about all around.

He hovered there, standing with the light of the hallway behind him so that all I could see was the sleek line of his shoulders. He wore a robe, Chinese in origin, like the rest of him, a bo staff in one hand. I'd bet my substantial comic book collection that he'd been practicing some kind of martial art. He wasn't sweating. Vampires, so far as I could tell, didn't sweat, but his hair was tucked up in some fancy braid to keep it out of his face.

"You just gonna stand there, or are you going to come in?" I didn't mean for it to sound sultry, but my still tired voice made it sound that way. "You just standing there makes me feel anxious."

He hesitated and then crossed the threshold into my room. He moved so nicely, like he was made of muscle and silk. He stepped a full foot into the room and then stopped.

"I had a nightmare," I said, realizing he was looking around the room for some kind of threat. "Just a nightmare."

His eyes flicked to me. "You are...unwell." For the first time, I heard a little lilt in his tone. In another person, it would have been a rush of concern.

I scoffed. "Gee, I can't imagine why that would be. Maybe because everyone has this grand opinion on what I need to be doing and whom I need to be doing it with. Maybe because, in the past three months, my entire life has changed. Maybe because I am struggling to figure out a plan for my own damn life. Should I just suck it up and have some prophecy baby? Damn my feelings. What does any of that matter? Should I just leave this town and never come back? I mean, I was doing fine with french fries and all that."

I hadn't expected all of that to spill, and from the look he was giving me, Wei hadn't expected it either. I couldn't figure out if we were close or not. We had lived together for three months (he, I, and his two vampiric brothers), but our closest moments had been while he was teaching me to fight.

"What do you need?"

I curled my knees up to my chin. My print pajama pants with vintage Wonder Woman pictures all over them bunched with the movement. What did I need? It was the most loaded question. This wasn't some fast food shift where I just needed to get into the groove of things. I needed...well, I needed a plan.

"We could practice."

He wasn't talking about magic. That, I practiced with Jenny and Marquessa. Reikah, a girl from the same cult that my mother and half-sister were a part of, had said, before I'd passed out, that she wished to help me learn magic as well. I didn't know how I felt about that, but I figure that all knowledge, no matter how different, is a good thing to learn.

Wei was talking about martial arts. Forms of Kung Fu, if we were going to get specific about it. I wasn't half bad. I wasn't all that great either, but I was learning. Even so, I was too worn-out for magic. Everything in me still hurt, and that weird dream had not left me feeling at all rested.

"Will you talk with me?"

He blinked. "Talk?"

I gave him a little smirk. "I know you can talk. I just...I need to figure out my plan, and I do better when I can talk it out."

"Alright."

Now that I had someone to talk to, my mind went a little blank. "Will you tell me how you became a vampire?"

He went very, very still. Most people's eyes went wide when they were surprised by something, or their eyebrows might go up their forehead. Wei went as still as a statue. He didn't even breathe. Vampires, after all, didn't have to breathe or eat, though most of them did the second one anyway.

"Why?"

I looked up at him. "Because you know an awful lot about me, and I know relatively little about you. Where were you born? When? Why did Vlad choose to make you one of his?"

He stayed so still for so long after that that I had to wonder if he was still alive, or as alive as an undead vampire can be.

"I was born in Yunnan Province, China, in your year of 1673."

I had to blow out a long breath. That made him just shy of three hundred and fifty years old. Impressive to say the least.

"Do you speak Chinese?"

"I do, but it is not my first language."

Now I was interested. Languages were cool. "What was?"

"Why?"

Well, that was a harder question to answer. I wanted to know because Wei was a bit of an enigma for me. I knew Alan well because the flamboyant vampire wore himself out for everyone to see. And I knew Dmitri because we both spoke the language of books and creativity; we had that in common. I didn't know Zane, the eldest of the vampire brothers, because I had been passed out for a good amount of the time that he had been back at the mansion since I had helped rescue him.

But mostly, I wanted to know Wei because I knew that he was in love with me.

Maybe that was weird, maybe a little childish, but there was a part of me that really liked the fact that he was interested in me. Then again, I remember hearing once that another person's interest was the greatest aphrodisiac.

"Didn't we just cover this?" I asked. "You know plenty about me. You know my name is Lorena Quinn, most recent legacy of the Quinn witches. You know that my mom is nuts and my dad was stupidly over protective. You know that my half-sister, Connie, pretended to be my friend so that she could help my mom kidnap me. You know that there is a prophecy about me and that I am obsessed with books and comics and video games."

I plucked at my Wonder Woman pajama pants, which were so worn in some places that the yellow W symbols were faded to almost white. I traced one of the symbols with the tip of one chipped nail and shrugged. "I know that your name is Wei, no surname given, and that you can beat things up pretty well."

I also knew that he had come charging to my rescue once they'd discovered where my mother had taken me, and that it had been Wei who'd been desperate to get me back. I had seen it in his face, felt it cross my skin. I was a necromancer, and that meant I had a little more insight into the undead mind than the average witch.

"Na." he said.

I raised my brow. "No what?"

A flicker of some emotion passed through his eyes. I think it was amusement. Wei? Amused with me? Certainly not. Wei was the master of the stone face, the man who felt little. That was what made him so untouchably cool.

"I did not say 'no.' I said 'Na.' Na is my surname."

"Wei Na?" I asked, trying out the name on my tongue.

"Na Wei," he corrected.

I couldn't help it. I giggled. Perhaps it was those couple of years that I spent in California, but the idea that his name was Na Wei tickled me. "It suits you."

"You are laughing at me."

"A little," I admitted, "but you rarely give me anything to laugh about; I'll take what I can get." I tugged a pillow into my lap and shifted until I could lean over it. "What can you tell me about the Yunnan province?"

He frowned at me and then shrugged. "What do you want to know? That it is in the southern part of China? That it was once taken over by the Mongols? That its past was a hard one, a difficult one, but that the people born there are strong and proud and brave? Or would you rather know that it was beautiful?"

He sounded almost wistful, I thought, as he began to describe his homeland. "There are many mountains and rivers. Years of growing rice on the sides of the mountains has carved hundreds of ledges that change colors with the seasons, where small fish and frogs gather in pockets of wetness. Women roll up their sleeves and wash off dirt in one of the hundreds of small waterfalls, and the men watch for birds that sing the songs of springtime."

I have to admit, I was a little caught up in it all. I didn't know that he could speak so poetically. "It sounds beautiful," I said, once I knew that he wasn't going to say more.

"It was then; I do not know if it is now. The world has changed many times since I was alive."

"You can sound so angsty; did you know that? Like, extra angsty."

"Angsty?"

I rolled my eyes. "I do not have the ability to explain the depth and complexity that is angst."

"I know the meaning of the word, but I don't think you mean it the way I define it."

I shrugged. "Must be the generational gap. When was the last time that you went out into the world?"

"When we went dancing."

"Oh, right." I don't know why I blushed with the memory of the way Wei had looked in a simple outfit of jeans and a shirt, but I did.

"What are you thinking about?"

I could have been coy and said "nothing" but I wasn't particularly good at coy. Awkward and socially inept, that I could do. "You."

He went still again. "What about me?"

"How you looked when we went out. It was a good look. Maybe you should wear that again, and I'd take you to the movies or something."

"Are you asking me on a date?"

I shrugged, surprised by my own forwardness. "A little. Unless you are going to tell me no; then I definitely wasn't asking you out, and you should feel ashamed for thinking such a thing." There was another flicker of amusement, and I considered myself on a roll. "You know, you don't have to keep hanging out in the doorway. You can come sit down."

Another hesitation, and then he moved further into the room. It took a little encouraging on my part, but I got him to sit on the edge of the bed. It made my heart beat just a little faster to think of Wei in my bed.

"Well?" he asked, tucking his legs neatly beneath his body.

"The Order...uhhh," I struggled to remember the name.

"Ordo Hermeticus Fidelis. The Order of the Loyal Hermit," Wei supplied.

I waved my hand in gratitude and nodded. "Yeah, them. The ones that think I should just walk away from all this, ignore the prophecy or maybe even hand it off to Connie...little unexpected half-sister. They truly think that it's better to keep magic locked up, that releasing it is tantamount to setting off a nuclear bomb."

"Do you agree?"

I had to think about that. Really think. I mean, I got where they were coming from. I really did. I was thinking about just unleashing magic. "I don't think so. I mean. On the one hand, I get where they are coming from. Magic is a power; it's a wildness, a creation. I dunno. It's not like I'm going to be handing everyone a gun...but I can see why they could think that."

"So, you want to fulfill the prophecy?"

I laughed. "Ever since I was a little girl, I dreamed of magic. I dreamed of a world where all the things I read about existed. I have that chance and that pretty much rocks. But..."

"But what?" he asked.

I sighed and wrapped my arms around my legs. The tears sprang into my eyes before I even realized I was going to cry about it. "But what if they are right? What if I'm just unleashing a weapon?"

The mattress moved beneath me, and a moment later, Wei's arms were around me. I collapsed against him and just started crying. I had never thought of myself as one of those people who cried when things got tough, but there I was.

"Anything coming from you could not be a weapon."

His voice was so soft, whispered right in my ear. I heard the softness of his accent. It sent an unexpected thrill down my spine.

I lifted my head and found myself looking into his face. At first glance, his eyes looked empty and emotionless, but I knew better. Wei hid everything about him beneath a layer of stillness. But this close, I could see there was something moving beneath those obsidian depths. It was only because I was watching him so carefully that I saw his gaze flick down to my lips.

My heart jumped.

My hand went to his cheek. It was warmer than I expected and soft. I had never known a guy to have such soft skin, but there it was. The golden tones of it made my fingers look pale, or maybe it was the other way around. There was the tiniest patch of hair on his chin, just a few shades lighter than the hair on his head, no wider than the pad of my thumb. I ran my finger across it, and his lips parted.

He was still beneath my touch, like a statue, as if he were afraid to move. I don't know why, but I was totally into it. I went up on my knees and laid the tiniest kiss on the broad line of his forehead, and still he stayed still. He didn't reach out for me. He didn't clutch or shift to make it easier. He simply let me touch him. I would have thought him utterly passive were it not for the way he seemed to vibrate beneath my hands. Every touch fed this ball of electricity that built inside my belly.

Everything in my life was so wild, so crazy. But here, in my room, with a thunderstorm rolling outside, he was a wave of calmness beneath my touch.

I bent my mouth to his, and the world seemed to shift. His lips were like satin beneath mine, warm and soft and pliant. For a moment, it was just my mouth moving against his. Then, his hands went to my hips, and the electricity turned to fire.

He levered himself up and over me, keeping our mouths fused together, and the next thing I knew, my back was against the bed. My arms went around him, and I drowned in the sensation of his kiss. I didn't know that this man, this vampire, could hide so much passion beneath that cool exterior. His hands were a blur along my skin, leaving a trail of flame in their wake.

I arched towards him, and he pushed against me; for a moment, I thought that I would burn. His mouth went lower down my neck, nipping along my skin. Then, I felt the brush of his teeth, and I knew they were fangs. Maybe there was something wrong with me, but right then and there? I was totally okay with it.

I turned my head, offering my neck to him, and I felt his teeth scrape along the skin. I shivered and made a sound that I had never made before. Everything in me felt alive, awake, and hungry. I had never felt quite like that before. I placed my hand on the back of his head and pulled him towards me. The sound that came out of his throat was more beast than human, and I liked it. I felt the barest press of his fangs against the fluttering in my throat. My free hand slipped inside the robe he wore, touching the skin of his stomach, feeling the lines of his body beneath.

I was absolutely sure that this was going to be it. That in a moment of unexpected passion, something incredible was going to happen. To be honest? I was totally ready for it. Maybe it was all the stress, all the pressure to choose or not choose or whatever. I pulled him to me and whimpered for more.

The next thing I knew, he was across the room. Not just pulled away, but all the way back at the door. His eyes, normally a deep obsidian, were a shade of ruby so bright they cast shadows across the room. His fangs were visible over the fullness of his lower lip. It was not a terrible look, but it was ruined by the shame splashed across his face. That look was better than a cold shower.

"What did I do?" I asked.

He didn't answer. He looked at me, sitting in the middle of rumpled sheets, in my equally rumpled pajamas, and whirled away like the creature of the night I knew him to be.

"What the hell?" I muttered, not sure if I was speaking to myself or the man who was no longer there.

It took me a full two minutes to get out of bed. I thought, at first, about going back to sleep. I even laid down and pulled the sheets back around me. But it was pretty much futile. All I could think about was how incredible I had felt and how awful it had turned.

Had I done something wrong? I couldn't say that I had the most hands-on knowledge of more intimate relationships, but I read enough fanfiction to know how everything was supposed to go. *This was not it. Right?* He had wanted me; I was pretty much sure of that, I thought, as I tossed back the coverlet and plodded over to the bathroom.

I looked in the mirror, wondering if something repulsive had happened to my face while I slept. Nope, same face I'd had all my life. Same ash-brown hair, same pointed nose. There was a yellowing bruise along my forehead and another on my shoulder. Maybe Wei just really disliked bruises? Yeah, I didn't think so. It had to be something else.

I looked a little lower at the tiny scrape on my neck. No, I decided, it wasn't a scrape. It was two pinpricks, like someone had bumped me ever so lightly with a bar-b-que fork. A tiny trail of blood had leaked out of one; the other wasn't even deep enough to offer that.

Is that what he freaked out about? Blood? Seemed a little weird for a vampire to be anti-blood. Or maybe that was the issue. Maybe he was really pro-blood. I remembered that look of shame on his face. Crap, he was freaked out about biting me. What the heck was that about? Then again, maybe I was wrong. I was human; a witch, sure, but human nonetheless. I could be wrong. It happened.

I turned the water on full blast and, while it was heating up, I sent a message to Jenny.

"Hey," the text read. "Have you ever had someone bail out on you right before getting to the good stuff?"

I hit send, stripped out of my pajamas and stepped under the spray. The hot water felt good on my muscles and pushed away the last bits of lust simmering under my skin. I needed a plan for the day, and part of that plan was to keep some distance between Wei and I because I just had no clue what to do about him.

In a flash of inspiration, I decided to switch from shower to bath. I wanted to soak, to think about everything. Not just about Wei, though the look on his face was going to be haunting the back of my mind for the next eternity or so. I added some of the multitude of bath salts to the water and watched the froth bubble up.

Two months ago, I'd never added expensive bath salts to the tub. Heck, in most of the super cheap apartments my dad had set us up in, there was rarely ever a tub involved in the first place. Cheap stand-up showers for everyone. Lounging in a bath had been a rare luxury.

Thinking of my dad chased away my worry about Wei. My dad hadn't called since our last conversation, the one where I had pretty much snapped at him. That worried me. He used to call every day. It used to be suffocating how much he had worried. But not hearing from him in three weeks? That was actually a little scary.

Great. Another thing to worry about. Maybe I should think about making a check list. Distant dad, weird mom, cult sister, prophecy baby, weird dreams, vampire boyfriend. While all of those might make for decent indie trash band names, they made for a daunting checklist. Add in learning magic and I was pretty sure that I was ready to pass everything off to someone else.

I slipped into the water, laying back my head, and asked myself the most important question any geeky girl could ask herself. What would Wonder Woman do?

My phone chimed, and I picked it up. Speaking of wonder woman...

The text from Jenny was short. "Sweetie, do you even know how many girls think they wanna smooch another girl until the shorts come off?"

She had a point. I wasn't a lesbian. I would probably never know what it was like to have someone I liked refuse my attentions because I had boobs. More often than not, I got attention because of my chest, not in spite of it. I sent a response along the lines of her deserving all the ladies in the world.

She said she'd settle for one.

"But it's not about me, prophecy girl; what happened? Who ran out on you? I need details."

I wasn't ready to give details. Mostly because I didn't know what the heck was going on with me. What was that dream about? Did it have meaning? Or was it just my subconscious working out the huge frag-fest that was my current life?

My phone went off again. I assumed it was Jenny. But the sender was marked as Unknown. I frowned. There were maybe seven people who had my cell phone number, and most of them were currently living under the same roof as me. I opened the message and frowned. It looked like gibberish to me, as if someone used emojis that my phone didn't understand. I couldn't quite ignore the sense of uneasiness as I closed the message, assuming that someone had sent the wrong person a text.

Whatever…there was just too much going on for me to worry about that kind of thing. Besides, my hands were starting to get wrinkly. I sent a final text to Jenny telling her that I needed some best buddy time and went off to find something to occupy my mind until I could get a little more sleep.

CHAPTER TWO

Ultimately, I decided to take some time for myself in the library. I loved the library. It was totally Beauty and the Beast. There was a big fireplace and shelves and shelves of all kinds of books. And when I couldn't figure out what was going on in my own life, I liked to turn to the literary world.

I wandered the shelves, letting my fingers glide over all the different books. Some were made of leather, some were cloth, and some were flimsy paperbacks. The collection was as varied as it was astonishing, and I loved it.

My father had moved us around a lot. I always thought that it had been because of work, but recently I had reason to believe that work was only part of it. I plucked my way through different sections of novels, remembering that, for the better part of my life, books and their cousins, comics, had been my best friends. That, I hoped, was changing, but only a little. Even so, there wasn't anyone I could chat with at two o'clock in the morning after a nightmare and the weirdest version of hot and cold ever. Too bad.

I picked up half a dozen novels and plopped myself into the world's most comfortable chair. I had a little bit of everything in my mini collection of novels, mostly because I didn't know what I really wanted to get into. Eventually, I settled on a book that I had already read before. There was something comforting about re-reading a novel, as if you were having a conversation with a friend.

I was just getting into it when I realized that someone was watching me.

I shouldn't have been surprised to see Dmitri there. After all, the library was as much his escape as it was mine.

"Hey," I said, using my thumb to mark the page I was on. "I didn't expect to see you up yet."

In fact, I hadn't expected to see him up at all. He'd been pretty badly wounded during the great escape from the compound of the Order. He looked tired, a little worn around the edges, but he was up and moving. He still looked a little out of it, and there was a paleness to him that I didn't like. I mean, he was a vampire, and therefore always pale, but this went a little too far.

He still continued to stand there and just stare at me, almost like he didn't expect to see me either. Maybe it was a trick of the light, but there was a brightness in his eyes that normally wasn't there.

"Is...is everything okay?"

He moved slowly towards me. There was something primal about his movements, as if he was some great hulking beast hunting down his prey. I felt my pulse jump, and not in a good way.

"Dmitri?" I asked, trying very hard not to let my voice quake.

He lifted his head, sniffing the air. His dark curls fell back, freeing his face. His ears weren't normal; they had points, and the tips of them had a glimmer of fur.

"Why do I smell Wei on you?" he asked, his voice like chipped gravel.

How the frick could he smell that? I'd taken a shower. I'd changed clothes. I mean, just how good was his sense of smell? But seriously, not my primary problem right now. "I really don't think that's any of your business." I probably sounded snippy, but I was feeling snippy. What right did he have to be jealous?

"Have you already chosen your mate?" he snarled.

Mate? What was this? Some weird alpha werewolf thing? No, thank you. I held up the book as a barrier between the two of us as he continued to creep forward.

"I haven't chosen anything, and you need to back off."

He sniffed the air again. "You believe what you say."

"Okay, what the hell is wrong with you?" I demanded. I didn't stand up, mostly because, if I did, I'd be closer to Dmitri, and right now, I didn't want that. I wanted a couple hours of reading so I could relax. Instead, I was dealing with a mantrum.

"He said he didn't want you. That he was not competing."

My temper, already short, popped. "Hey, listen buddy. I'm not a prize. I'm not handing out medals. I'm participating in this little thing because I wasn't given a whole lot of choice. It was either do this or let people die out."

It was true enough. It had been thoroughly explained to me that without magic, those people attached to magic, like vampires, elves, werewolves, and who knew what else, would slowly die. It's why there were only the better part of a dozen vampires in the world when there could have been a few thousand. It was also why everyone was really hard on me to pick a baby-daddy or whatever the term was.

"He wasn't supposed to want you."

Well, that was just rude. I resisted the urge to slap him with the book, partly because he was beginning to shift in front of me and that was pretty much terrifying. His mouth grew longer and more bestial, and his eyes shimmered with an angry light. Claws formed on the ends of his fingers, and my flight or fight response was still loading in the back of my mind.

"I..." I had to swallow around the lump of fear that had grown in my throat. "I don't know what he wants. I just..."

"Liar!" He snapped and dove forward. I scrambled backwards, inhibited by the shape of the chair.

It's funny. All the movies I had ever watched and all the books I had ever read depicted brave heroines making these awesome leaps or elegant steps out of harm's reach. Me? I scrambled like some kind of petrified crab over one of the arms and slithered between the stacks of books in the hopes that some space would do the both of us good. My carefully curated pile of books fell to the ground. I'm pretty sure I made some kind of protesting squeak. There was absolutely nothing elegant about it.

"Dmitri, what the hell is wrong with you?"

"I want you." He snarled it; all the words were said with teeth and snapping. "You should be mine."

Yeah, no. I didn't think so. Making a girl terrified did not equate to being attracted to her. That was some creepy red flag stuff. Some chicks were into that. Me? No, thanks. I, apparently, preferred guys who couldn't figure out what they wanted.

The shelf to my right shuddered as a weight slammed into it. I could only assume it was Dmitri. A moment later, his shadow loomed, and I realized I had run further into the room rather than out of it as I had intended. He was bigger and faster and a whole lot angrier than I was. Any move I could make, he could make faster.

"Why?" I demanded, as it was the only question going through my mind. "Why should I be yours?"

It was, apparently, a really difficult question. His head, more animal now than human, cocked to one side like some great big dog. His eyes flickered as if he was stuttering through whatever thought process I had started.

"You like me."

I resisted the urge to roll my eyes. I did not think being flippant was going to help me at all in this situation. "So? I like a lot of people."

Apparently, my mouth thought flippant was the way to go. Awesome.

He snarled. No, that wasn't right. Dogs snarled. This sound was not human, but it wasn't even bestial. It rumbled like speakers with too much bass, like a dozen wolves in the valley between mountains. His teeth were pricks of white against a wild darkness. I watched them move as the snarl morphed into a howl.

I had never had that kind of response to a relatively simple question, and I used to work fast food.

He grabbed one shelf with his clawed hand, and it vibrated with the strength of the movement. The wood squeaked a protest.

"Why...not...me?" Each word was punctuated, carefully spoken, mostly because he didn't seem to have human lips anymore.

This was not the first time a nice guy had asked why I wasn't interested in him. It was, however, the first time that my lack of interest wasn't ultimately true. I liked Dmitri. I thought he was fun to hang out with. I liked hearing him read. I liked the way he smiled. I didn't *not* like him. I was just having a lot of feelings for Wei that was taking me by surprise, and I didn't really know what to do with that.

"I haven't picked!" I finally snapped around the ball of fiery fear that I was choking on. "I haven't picked anything. We kissed!"

Okay, that wasn't fair; it was a lot more than a kiss, but I really didn't think that Dmitri needed to know that. I was allowed to have some privacy.

It was also, apparently, the wrong thing to say. He howled. It was a wild, angry sound that shook dust from the tops of the shelves. I ran. It was stupid and blind, but I ran. Tears, unwanted and frustrating, ran out of my eyes, and I stumbled out of the sanctuary of the bookshelves and back towards the sitting area. My slippered feet slid across the slick wooden floors, offering me little to no help in my escape. Moments later, I became a stereotype; I took a bad step and tumbled to the ground. My knee hit first, a brilliant shock of pain leaving me temporarily blind.

Dmitri was over me like a shot, or I should say the animal with Dmitri's face was. He had grown. Normally, he was a little over six feet tall and built like a linebacker. Now, he was more like a seven-and-a-half-foot tall Mr. Universe covered in rich dark hair. If not for the fangs as long as my thumbs sticking out of his mouth, I would have thought he was a werewolf, not a vampire.

His breath was hot on my face as his nose flared, taking in my scent. I didn't know what fear smelled like, but the look on his face told me he wasn't turned off. Oh, boy. I squirmed back as much as I could, but my back met the relentless line of a wall, and I knew I was doomed. Goodbye, prophecy. I wasn't going to make it.

"Dmitri," I whispered. "Please stop."

He bent his head and pressed his nose to my neck, taking in a deep breath. "Want," he growled.

I don't know what would have happened next. One moment, Dmitri was over me, his breath on my face, and the next, he made a sound like a kicked dog. The enormous presence of him disappeared, and I could breathe again.

I expected to see Wei. I don't know why, but I did. Instead, Zane, tall and dark, stood over me, holding Dmitri in one hand at the back of the neck like a very bad dog. The last time I had seen Zane, he had looked like a guy who had just woken up from a twenty-year-long coma, skinny and sunken-eyed. The man who stood there now was not those things. He was the very essence of empowerment. His muscles still had a lanky grace to them, but the definition was incredible. His dark hair had been pulled into neat braids, falling just to his ears. His eyes were bright gold, like a hawk's, and glittered angrily.

He wasn't the only angry one.

Dmitri snarled and tugged against the grip, lashing out with his claws. I don't know what happened, but he never hit. He should have. Dmitri was no slouch in the fighting department, but everywhere that those animalistic claws struck out turned to a shadowy mist.

"Stop," Zane's deep voice boomed. It wasn't just that he had a voice worth of James Earl Jones; there was a power to it. Dmitri went still, and so did I. His eyes flicked up to see me, and he gave me a look full of a meaning I couldn't interpret in my state. "Relax."

It was as if I had just received a ten-hour massage. All the fear I had drained, and then a little more until I was little more than a boneless mass sitting on the library floor. Dmitri was no better, though his change was a little more wild...or maybe less wild, since he went from that animal hybrid form to something more human.

"What the hell?" I asked.

"We are the Sons of Vlad, created in the mirror of his image" Zane said as if that made perfect sense. "Dmitri is the aspect of the beast."

I struggled to try to remember what had been told to me, what I had read in my grandmother's grimoire, or book of magical knowledge. The sons of Vlad, a term for the vampire offspring of Vlad Dracul, the first vampire, were aspects of him. I knew, thanks to certain authors and the binge watching of several vampire shows, that Dracula had a lot of special talents.

He could change his appearance, either to be beautiful or terrifying, or not be seen at all. He could call to animals. He could scale walls and all of that too. Perhaps I hadn't thought about the fact that his sons, or offspring, whatever you wanted to call them, couldn't do everything that he could do. They had their own talents, or rather, they could do one of Vlad's talents really well.

Dmitri, apparently, got all the animal traits. I wasn't too sure about what everyone else could do.

"And you?"

Zane's smile was slow and not altogether kind. "I am the shadow."

Okay. Yeah. Sure. That made a whole lot of sense.

"Lorena?" Dmitri's voice sounded harsh, as if he had a sore throat. Maybe howling did that to a guy. I didn't know.

"You should not speak with her." Zane kept a firm hold on the back of Dmitri's neck. "You have lost that privilege."

"I...I didn't...I..." He hung his head in shame. I almost felt sorry for him until my knee gave a throb. "I came in to visit, and I smelled him on her."

"Jeez," I said, pushing a hand through my hair. Way to call me out.

"I didn't expect it. I... was angry."

"Why?" I asked. I would have sounded a lot angrier if the magic of Zane's voice wasn't still a comfortable blanket on me.

Dmitri hung his head. He muttered something I couldn't hear. Zane gave him a shake.

"Is that necessary?"

Zane raised his eyes to mine. The look he gave me was easier to understand. He was saying that I was being stupid. Maybe I was. I just didn't like to see people hurt, even if they hurt me. Empathy was weird.

"It is," Dmitri said. He hung his head even lower, until his rich curls formed a curtain over his face. "I hurt you."

I wasn't going to argue with that. He totally had. "Why? I mean, I don't understand. Why do you care?"

"Alan has made it clear that you were not going to choose him," Zane said when Dmitri stayed silent.

Well, that was news to me. Yeah, it was true enough that I considered Alan out of the running. After all, he was completely, one hundred percent, in love with Dmitri. It was hard for me to have warm, fuzzy feelings when I knew I was always going to be second best in his eyes. But that didn't mean that I had decided on Dmitri. I hadn't decided on anything really.

"So let me get this straight. Alan made it clear, and you decided that you were going to…what? Come in here and claim your prize?" Suddenly, the calm feeling evaporated, and I was on my feet. "You thought that, since you see me as some kind of trophy, you could just come in here and take what was yours by default?"

"I…that wasn't my intent. I came to speak with you, and then I smelled him."

"Who or what I smell like is none of your damn business." I spread my arms wide. "I don't care if I smell like a sweaty football team and half the cheerleaders. I don't care if I smell pure as the driven snow. You can keep your nose to yourself. Do you hear me?"

"Have you chosen him?" he asked. He sounded like I'd kicked him. Even with how mad I was at him, it was heartbreaking to hear.

I shoved my fingers through my hair. I hadn't chosen Wei. It had just been a moment, a random, crazy, hormone-filled moment, and I wasn't going to be cornered with making any kind of decision when my feelings were on super max. No, sir.

"I need to get out of here."

"That isn't a good idea." Zane's voice was a gentle roll, like distant thunder.

"You know what bothers me even more than someone sniffing out my personal business? People saying that me going out isn't a good idea. Me leaving, right now, is what's best for everyone."

"I-" Dmitri started.

I did not want to hear it. It didn't much matter if he agreed with me or not. Right this moment, his opinion mattered less than the next fight between Batman and the Wallflower; no one cared. I pushed past them. This time, I didn't forget my magic. I wasn't terrified out of my mind. I was pissed.

My magic flowed out of me and wrapped around them like a glove. It was so easy. So simple to just fling them back and away from me. I had never cast something so easily. It didn't take words or a lot of thought or herbs and ritual. All it took for me was to know that they were the undead, and I was a necromancer. I heard books crash, but I didn't look back. I was swimming in my own power, and it was like being drunk.

I went up to my room and hauled my big satchel bag out from its hiding place under my great big four poster bed. *No,* I thought, *not mine. This place wasn't mine.* This mansion belonged to a bunch of vampires, Sons of Vlad, whatever the heck they wanted to call themselves. I didn't belong here. This was nuts. Right?

In a flurry of confusion, I began shoving things into my bag. Anything and everything that felt right, regardless of whether or not I would need it.

What the hell was happening tonight? I had just begun to get out of bed after what could only be called an epic battle, and I had nearly gone to third base, been assaulted, and then been emotionally manipulated. It was too much too fast, and I just didn't have the strength for it. I needed to get out, and I needed to get out now.

There was a polite knock on my bedroom door. For a moment, I thought it was Wei; then, I realized that Wei probably wouldn't have knocked, politely or otherwise.

"What?"

The door opened, and Alan stood there.

Alan, I had thought, looked like the perfect fallen angel. His golden blonde hair hung longer than mine had ever been. His face was a play of softness and angles that gave him a particular attractiveness that I could only define as masculine beauty. Like the quintessential vampire that he was, his clothing, tonight in shades of blue velvet, spoke of old French aristocracy. Funny, considering when he'd been alive, he'd been a French peasant.

"I heard of...what happened."

"Which part?"

His smile was slow. "I heard of Dmitri's...impropriety."

"That's a fancy term for attack."

Alan sighed softly. When I looked at him, I saw his mask of perfect politeness slip and a flicker of raw emotion shine through. When he was thinking about it, Alan had a tendency to look mildly amused at everything; his lips were perpetually smirking, and his eyes always had a slight impish shine to them. But I knew better. Alan and I had gone on a few outings, but none had helped me understand him more than our trip to France when he'd shown me where he grew up. I had also known, before the night was out, that Alan would never love me because he was too in love with Dmitri.

Well, he can have him, I thought. The thought, vivid and visceral as it was, had me going still. Had I already chosen?

No, I decided. I hadn't chosen anything. I was too close to the guys. Too close to this house and the melodrama of all this crap. I had come to Virginia with one goal. I was going to live in my grandmother's house and learn who and what I was. I was going to figure out what I wanted in life, and all of that had been messed up when an elderly witch had told me about a prophecy that involved not just me, but the child I would eventually have.

Well, screw that. Right this moment, that child was the most distant desire in my mind. All I wanted was some time to myself.

"Dmitri cannot always control his baser instincts."

"That's on him. I shouldn't have to put up with it. I'm not the one that's in love with him."

Alan didn't flinch. He went still. Perfectly and utterly still. Humans couldn't be that motionless. He didn't breathe, didn't blink. Not a single muscle moved. He was a statue. I knew what I had said really bothered him.

I sighed. "I'm sorry. You haven't done anything wrong, and I'm lashing out."

He was still for another moment, and then he hugged me. It was a slow thing, filled with velvet and lace and strength. It was an interesting person that could go from being offended to hugging in a matter of seconds. I couldn't have done it.

"These weeks have not been easy on you. I'd be more surprised if you didn't need a vacation from it." He gave me a little squeeze. "Where will you go?"

There was only one place where I could be safe, where I could learn more about me. "My grandmother's."

He nodded and placed a single chaste kiss on my forehead. "A wise enough choice. May I visit?"

I hugged him tighter. He was so slender that it was so easy for me to wrap around him even as he did the same with me. "Of course."

We stood like that for another minute, and then my phone went off. It was Jenny asking what I needed. I smiled. For all the crap going on in my life, how great was it to have a friend who asked what I needed at two thirty in the morning?

I sent a single message: "Pizza and video games?"

The response was a slew of emojis that told me she was all for it.

Alan placed a finger under my chin and tilted my head up to look into his ridiculously beautiful face. "I do not wish to place an even greater burden on you, but remember that even while you take this vacation that there are still three men waiting here for you."

I frowned. "I thought we decided that you were out of the running?"

He smiled and pressed a single finger to my lips. "While I will hardly explain to you that love isn't necessary to create a child, you are correct. We have decided that I am not for your bed. However, I am not speaking of myself."

I don't know why it took me forever to put two and two together, but it totally did. Then, a handsome face popped into my head with a voice like liquid gold. "Zane?"

Alan nodded slowly. "He doesn't appeal to you?"

I shrugged. "Alan, he's very cute, but...but I don't know him."

"A few weeks ago, you didn't know any of us."

CHAPTER THREE

We were in our third hour of a Next Top Model binge watching session. It was not my first choice in entertainment, but when you had a friend, sometimes you watched what they wanted because seeing them happy made even the most catty conversations worth watching.

"You could be a model," I told Jenny as I stuffed a pizza crust, dipped in ranch dressing, in my mouth.

"Shut up," she said, poking me with one toe.

"You could, though," I said. I meant it. Jenny was quite possibly the prettiest girl I had ever seen. Being sleek and tall and graceful was a big help, but more than that, Jenny had this awareness of self that I think would have looked perfect on some glossy pages or strutting down the runway. "You could take the world of fashion by storm." It wasn't my best Tyra Banks impression, but I tried.

Jenny snorted. "Oh my god, you are such a dork."

I shrugged. As far as I was concerned, being a dork was a compliment. "And the world broke with the truth of that statement."

Jenny laughed. It was a good sound. Then, she went quiet and stretched out on my grandmother's couch, one foot, clad in a bunny slipper, bounced thoughtfully. "You think I could be a model?"

"Heck yes," I said.

She shook her head. "They'd never let it happen. A black lesbian witch as a model?"

"Well, they don't have to know about the witch part." I flopped back against the mountain of pillows I had crafted for myself. "In fact, it's probably better that they don't."

She snorted. "It's probably best if they think I'm straight and white too, but that ain't gonna happen."

"Get up then! Show me that walk."

"No!" Jenny pulled a pillow over her face, smothering another laugh. "I can't do that."

"Why not? Are you embarrassed? My Jenny? Queen of everything in this world and probably a few smaller universes."

She threw the pillow at me, and I ducked. It slapped against the other pillows and tumbled into my lap. I wrapped my arms around it and tugged it close.

"You think I could?" she asked again.

"I wouldn't have said it if I didn't. I am a lot of things, but a kind liar isn't one of them."

She laughed. "You do tell the truth. Tell me again what you told to Dmitri. What was it? You don't care if you smell like a whole football team?"

"I think I threw in some cheerleaders for variety, but yeah." I plucked a forkful of Oreo fluff and popped it into my mouth. There was nothing like Oreo fluff after a crappy night.

She rolled over on her belly and kicked her feet into the air. "Tell me the truth. What was it like with Wei?"

I shook my head. "Oh no. No no no. You gotta do the walk first."

"Hah! What? You wanna trade my runway walk for your dirty details?"

"Heck yes I do."

Tyra Banks was talking about behavior and sensuality on the television. I could see Jenny thinking it over.

"Alright, fine. Let's do this."

She jumped up and strutted down the short hallway between the front bedroom and the back bedroom. I don't know what I was expecting, but the incredible strut in a pair of fluffy bunny slippers and rubber ducky pajamas was not it. She runway walked in a way that made everything bounce and bobble and, by the end of it, I was sure that she could be America's next top model.

Then, she ruined it by stepping in the Oreo cream pie we'd gotten from the 24-7 mart.

"Aaack!" she cried out. "Not my bun-bun."

I blinked. "Did...did you name your slipper?"

"Cold water!"

I went to the kitchen sink and started running cold water. She took the vegetable scrubber, shaped like a row of tomatoes, and began to clean off her slipper.

"It was great," I said.

"Huh?"

"With Wei. It was great. Like, I've had make-out sessions before. I've enjoyed some people, but it's never been like that. That was something else entirely. That was...it was good."

She smirked at me, and plopped her wet slipper in the sink. "So why didn't you just go for it? Why not just...enjoy him, maybe put the nail in the coffin of this prophecy?"

"I nearly did," I admitted. "But he jumped away from me like he had touched something gross. As if I was a great big Oreo pie that he had stepped in. Like, one moment, his hands are all over my goodies, and the next, he is literally back across the room, using his super human speed to get the heck away from me. Like...I've had people say that they weren't into me, but I've never had someone dash away from me like friggen Spider Man."

"Are you serious?"

"One hundred percent. I mean. What the hell? I was into it. Like, Jesus. He kisses like how I imagine Clark Kent would kiss."

Jenny gave me a look. "You've imagined Superman kissing you?"

"Heck, yeah. Have you seen that farm boy smile? I'm all for that. And that protective boy scout attitude? All those Batman fangirls can keep their emo bad boy. I'll take the good guy any day."

"I'll take Wonder Woman, thanks. And not just because she's basically the most badass female to ever be. She's got this whole...I dunno...princess thing going on. I dig that. Besides, she grew up on an island of women; don't' tell me she only digs on dudes."

I giggled. "Fair."

"So, what are you going to do about Wei?"

"Nothing," I answered.

She looked unsure. "Nothing?"

I shrugged and plopped back down on my mountain of pillows, drawing my legging-clad knees up to my chin. "You know what? I'm not going to chase after him. He's got crap to work out; he can work it out. He wants to see me? He can come here."

"You tell him." Jenny offered me a high five. I took it.

She plopped herself back down on the couch. "It's like...six in the morning, and neither of us has gotten any sleep."

I frowned. "Wait. Why the heck are you still up?"

She didn't answer at first. Instead, she pulled off her remaining bunny slipper and tossed it on the ground. "Reikah."

Reikah was another witch. Maybe witch wasn't the right word. As far as I could tell, witchcraft was organic. It was about rituals, sure, but there was something flowing and intuitive about its practice. Reikah was far more rigid than that. There was something mathematical about the way she used magic. A mathe-magician.

I rolled over to give Jenny my full attention. "Wait, what about Reikah?"

"She's....really pretty."

I thought about that. Reikah had that Indian beauty thing going on. Long black hair and darker eyes and a sort of effervescent elegance that I couldn't put my finger on. Yeah, she was beautiful, but she hadn't said more than two or three words to me since she had helped me escape the compound for the Cult that she had belonged to, which had been weird because until very, very recently she'd been living two doors down from me at the mansion.

"Do you two...talk?"

Jenny shrugged and looked away. I took that to mean that there was some talking.

"You little hussy!" I said, tossing the recently thrown pillow back at her. "Why haven't you told me anything?"

Jenny caught the pillow and pressed it over her face. "Ugh! Because there ain't a thing to tell. I mean, we have talked, but there ain't nothing like...flirty." I wondered if she knew her rural Virginia accent became more audible when she was embarrassed. Probably. Jenny knew herself pretty well.

"Well then, what do you talk about?"

"Magic," she said with a roll of her golden-brown eyes. "Don't get me wrong. I am all for talking about magic. But she has this strict way of looking at it, and she's just...you know...a li'l bit full of herself."

"And you being the queen of modesty," I teased.

She gave me the tiniest smirk. "Shut up. You act like you know who I am."

I stuck my tongue out at her. "I totally know who you are. We are best friends."

She placed a dramatic hand over her heart. "Oh, now you are gonna make me tear up."

"You aren't allowed to do that!" I said, surging to my knees. "Whatever will I do?"

We held our overly dramatic poses for a whole ten seconds before we toppled over and deteriorated into enthusiastic giggles. Or maybe they were just exhausted giggles. After all, the sun was starting to come up over the mountain, and neither one of us had gotten any sleep.

"Alright," I said, flopping back on my pillow pile. "I should sleep."

"What?" she asked as I pulled a blanket over my legs. "Out here?"

I frowned. "Where else would I sleep?"

She used her long leg and now bare toe to point towards my grandmother's room. "That's your place, Hon."

CHAPTER FOUR

I dreamed again. I wasn't in the car this time, but sitting at a table. It could have been any table sitting in any room in any white-walled place in America. There were no decorations and nothing that felt like a home. Just a blank slate on top of pale gray carpet. I sat in one chair, wearing a pair of jeans, faded and comfortable, and a hoodie for a college I had never gone to. I knew, in the way that you know in dreams, that I wasn't alone.

At first, I didn't see her; I just felt the overwhelming knowledge of her distinct presence. After all, my relationship with my mother was almost entirely ethereal in nature.

The moment I thought the word *'mother,'* I could see her. Again, she was wearing the gray robes that I knew her to favor, without any accessories or stylization to make them stand out. The *Ordo Hermeticus Fidelis,* more commonly referred to as The Order of the Loyal Hermit, was the cult my mom belonged to. And, for that matter, so did my half-sister.

As soon as I thought of her, there she was too. She wasn't sitting at the table; instead, she was standing in a doorway I hadn't really seen before. At her feet was a giant dog, like a wolf but with a pointed, more vicious face. It leaned protectively against her. I wasn't surprised; animals were for her what the undead were for me: a connection to my magic. It surprised me, I think, that someone who belonged to an order who believed in strict practice in the realm of magic was connected with animals, who I thought of as the epitome of organic. Then again, what did I know? I hadn't even been practicing for a quarter of a year.

"What are you doing?" my mother asked.

"Sleeping," I answered, knowing it was true. I may have said it a little snippily, but I was feeling a little overwhelmed to even be looking at her. What the heck was the woman who had manipulated and kidnapped me to her little cult compound, run by her Jim Jones boyfriend, doing in my dream? "What do you want?"

She sat back, the hood of her robes masking a face that I knew to be beautiful and completely unlike mine. "To say I'm sorry."

I hated that I wanted to believe her. It wasn't a big part of me, just a tiny little part, the size of a germ, but it happened. This minuscule hope that my mom wasn't a terrible human being, that she cared about me, and that she didn't just think of me as the daughter that she shouldn't have had. A part of me still clung to the dream that I had a mom that loved me. Stupid, yeah, but true.

"Sorry?" I asked.

"I can apologize. I'm a person, not a monster." She sounded a little offended.

It might have been the worst possible thing that she could have said. "You're right. Only a monster would use magic to manipulate her eldest daughter to go to a cult compound."

"We aren't a cult," Connie said. She sounded offended too. If this was my dream, why was everyone arguing with me? I liked the dreams where we all agreed and then went diving in swimming pools full of ice cream while dinosaurs danced to salsa music in the background. These hyper surrealistic arguments with the family I had barely found out I had just weren't doing it for me.

"Cults," my mother said, going back to her unruffled tone, "strip away your identity; they take away who and what you are, make you feel important, powerful."

It was my less than professional opinion that my mother's little magic club was doing just that. I didn't have all the details on it yet, but I eyed the twin robes that my mother and sister wore, completely lacking in personality. Taking away identity? Check. Feeling special? Well, that was totally their shtick too. Magic, according to their order, was relegated to the few, not the masses. While I understood what they were saying in theory, history told us over and over again that leaving power in the hands of only a couple of people was the fast track to riot-ville. So that was a check too.

Yup. Definitely a cult.

I sat back in my dream chair, and it shifted. It was no longer cheap plywood and particle board with a stiff cushion. It was a dark wood throne with curling armrests. It was a position of power and, I gotta admit, I liked how it felt beneath me.

"I'm not going to argue this with you," I said with a shake of my head. My ash brown hair had been arranged into curls, pulled back with a tiara of diamonds that glittered with every movement. My pajamas shifted into a rich gown of velvet, the same shade of blue-gray-green as my eyes were. "You sit there and you tell me that you want to apologize, but already you are trying to make excuses for what you did."

"You have to understand-"

I rolled my eyes. "No, I don't. I know everyone says it's the adult thing to do to just let people be and let them have their own thoughts so long as those thoughts aren't hurting anyone, but, Mom, you hurt me. And you wanna keep magic locked up in this neat little ball that only you and your friends practice, and I don't think I'm okay with that."

"Would you offer nuclear weapons to everyone?" Connie demanded. The dog at her feet snapped its teeth at me. They were sharp, too sharp for a normal dog.

I rolled my eyes. "Let's not go down that path, okay?"

"Why?" my mother wanted to know. She still sounded calm, but there was a gleam in her eyes as if she had caught me in my own web. "Because it bears a ring of truth?"

I sighed. This was a conversation that I really just didn't want to have. It wasn't that I couldn't argue my side of it. I had spent enough years in customer service to learn when to just shut up and let a person say whatever they wanted. I had also learned how to put my views in a clear and concise manner (thank you, three years on the public high school debate team), and I knew that I didn't want to walk down this path...but I was totally going to do it anyway.

"No," I said flatly. "It doesn't."

Connie rolled her eyes. The dog growled. My mother, however, looked at me with a steadfast curiosity that was almost amusing; you know, if it hadn't been directed at me.

"How so?"

I blew out a long breath. I sat up straight, not because I thought I was better than my mom, though I pretty much believed I was, but because sometimes you had to get a little full of yourself to get your point across. The sleeves of my dream gown slithered over the arm rests as I folded my hands in front of me. "It's a bad comparison. No, it's a crap comparison. A nuclear bomb has one ability. It's destroys. It falls out of the sky, gives this big ol' blast of EMP, which wrecks technology, and then it obliterates an area of life and everything in it.

Then, you know what? It lingers. If the bomb is big enough and bad enough, it doesn't even allow for regrowth after that because is screws up the area so badly. But you know what? The same can't be said for magic. Magic has the ability to protect. It has the ability to help things grow. It has the ability to heal. Yeah, it can hurt people. No argument there. But at the end of the day, it's more complex than comparing it to a stupid nuclear bomb."

I hadn't even known that was my view until the words started pouring out of my mouth. Yeah, at first, I had been okay with the magic=weapon idea, but now? No. I had dipped my toes into the possibilities of magic and knew better.

Connie's lip curled into a wolfish snarl. My mother's mouth settled into a bemused grin. She almost looked proud. Then again, maybe that was just my inner child wishing really hard.

"An interesting view. But let us say that there are only one or two of the people who inherit magic because of your fulfillment of this prophecy. What about all the deaths that they accomplish?"

It was my turn to roll my eyes. Even for a dream, that was a cheesy line of thought. "Is this the blood on my hands speech? Because if it is, you lose major cool points. Sad because you don't have all that many to start off with. But again, I'm going to have to say no. If I give someone something, anything, and they use that to kill someone, it's not my fault. That death is on them."

"Even if you know that they could use it as a weapon?" Connie demanded.

"Seriously, in this day and age, anything can be used as a weapon. Someone assaulted an old woman with a loaf of bread the other day. Is it the bakery's fault? Nope. It's on the shoulders of the person who committed the assault. Plain and simple."

"So why not just give everyone a gun?"

I rolled my eyes again. I did not want to stay on this soapbox in my dreams, but it didn't look like I was going to be awake anytime soon. "Uugh. We already covered this. Guns have only one ability. To hurt. That's it. That's all they can do. Let's use a better comparison here. Let's use a Swiss Army Knife, the multi-tool of doom. A tool that can help you survive in the right circumstances. Then, let's say that we can attach a smart phone and a personal doctor to that SWK. I'm all for giving everyone one of those. That's awesome. Leaving that tool in the hands of just a few is, as far as I can tell, creating a class system that we don't need."

"How liberal of you," my mother said. Now, she didn't sound proud.

I shrugged. "Maybe a little. But I work fast food. You tend to get pretty liberal after being stuck in minimum wage for four years."

Connie scoffed. I was surprised she was being so vocal in my dreams. Usually, she was quiet.

"Well then, that settles it."

"Settles what?" I said. My mother had sounded pretty fatalistic.

"You'll have to die." She drew her hand down the table. Her fingers made an intricate pattern so quick my eyes couldn't follow. But I could see the trail her fingers made. They created a glowing circle on the wood, split into three perfect sections. Symbols I didn't understand shimmered between the lines both inside the circle and outside. Watching the swim of light made me nauseous.

Okay. I totally wanted to wake up now. I told my body to be conscious, but it was like pulling away from cold molasses. The dream sucked me down.

"What are you doing?" I demanded. I felt sick to my stomach. Everything was swimming. The walls weren't white anymore. They were the same acid green as the magic my mother used, the same color as the storm in my first weird dream. Not cool. "Back off."

I threw up my hands. I knew I could create a magical barrier. I pictured a perfect glass ball around me, like a great big hamster ball but only half as adorable. My magic pushed into it, but it didn't feel like glass; it felt like a bubble, pliable and easily broken. My mother reached out a hand. The symbol she had drawn on the table echoed in her palm.

The dog howled. The bubble broke. And I screamed as a pain I had no chance of describing ripped right through me.

"Lorena!" I heard a voice from a very long way off. I really wanted to follow it.

"What are you doing?" I asked again.

"I really hoped that we could be close," my mother said. "I'm sorry."

Weird, I thought as I felt a pounding behind my eyes, she didn't sound all that sorry. She sounded happy. The inner child in me, the one who had hoped with everything she had that my mom might not be a wholly terrible person, threw a tantrum.

How dare she! Because we had a difference of opinion on magic, she was going to…what? Kill me? Nope. Not gonna happen. I had stuff to do. I had a prophecy to fulfill and some fuzzy feelings to figure out. This whole death thing was just not going to work out for me.

Anger, hot and wild, swam through my veins. It burned away the pain behind my eyes, the sickness in my stomach. It burned like a forest fire, obliterating all the unwanted and leaving nothing in its wake. For a split second, I saw the flash of eyes like volcanic glass glimmering at me from the distance of consciousness.

Then, the strangest thing happened. I heard a cat yowl. It echoed through the dreamscape and seemed to clear the last bits of confusion from my mind. When it was done, I felt cold. More than that, I felt powerful. Magic spilled through me, gathering in my palms like a phantom wind. I got up out of my dream throne and hurled one hand at my mother, and one at my sister.

This was my dream, I screamed inside my own head, and I was master here. My mother let out a gasp as she slammed against the wall. She disappeared in a wisp of gray smoke. Moments later, my sister did the same. The dog went with her.

"Lorena!" the voice called again.

I woke up with a hiss of pain. Dear god, everything hurt. I felt like I had run fifteen miles after completing some Mr. Universe triathlon. I was made of rubber, warm rubber. I was burning up and cold all at once. The pillow beneath my head was soaked with sweat.

Jenny stood over me. Her eyes were wide with fear. I could smell salt and earth. Those were Jenny's elements. "Hold on!" she cried out, taking my face between two very warm hands. "Grandma's on the way."

Oh good, I thought because my mouth couldn't form the words. I was glad someone was coming who might be able to help. Because if I had to go on living like this, the chances of me actually being able to do that whole prophecy thing were slim to none.

CHAPTER FIVE

Marquessa Green was beautiful in the way that only older women could be. You just didn't get that kind of elegance and confidence before you hit the mid-thirties. Her mahogany face with its honey highlights stared down at me with all the warmth and compassion that a woman with multitudinous grandchildren could have. The last time I had seen her, she had her salt and pepper hair, more pepper than salt, in the natural tight curls of a woman of African descent. Some capable fingers had coiled those into a series of complicated braids that formed a woven crown around her head. Someone had stuck some flowers in the crown too. I thought that was neat. More older women ought to wear flower crowns.

"How do you feel?" she asked.

I still couldn't answer. I managed, just barely, to let my head fall to the left and the right in a slow yet exaggerated 'no'.

"That bad, huh?" she asked. Her Appalachian voice was twice as thick as her granddaughter's. "Seems 'bout right. Nearly got your soul ripped out of your body. Can't much think of anything that will hurt like that."

My soul? If my body, still feeling like a hundred and thirty pounds of half-melted putty, had been capable, I would have shivered. As it was, I just sank a few more centimeters into the net of blankets and quilts that Jenny had tucked me into. I was grateful for it. I had been pretty cold.

"Alright," Marquessa said, pulling up a large bag. The scent of herbs swarmed me, and I felt all the better for it. "Well then, let's see what we can do."

She began to hum a soft song with the tempo of a lullaby. Her hands, covered in an herbal cream, touched my brow.

"Jenny," she said.

My best friend (and savior as far as I could tell) leaned over me. She placed a stone on my forehead. Magic radiated through me. Jenny started to hum too. Her song was different, but it seemed to mesh with Marquessa's. They placed another bit of cream and a stone on my lips, my throat, on my chest, solar plexus, belly, and over that place where period cramps happen. With each stone, I felt a little better.

I wasn't sure if this went on for minutes or hours. Time didn't seem to have a whole lot of meaning right then. I was just a body that felt half-formed and barely there, boneless and exhausted. I let them work their magic. I think, at some point, I slept. Because when I woke up, the stones were gone and I was feeling a whole lot better.

I sat up, which was definitely a step in the right direction. My head spun, and I felt weak, but I could move.

"Well, now," Marquessa said. "There you are."

I was in my grandmother's room, the big comfortable bed nested high with pillows and blankets. Marquessa, wearing a pair of comfortable pants and a loose shirt, looked me over. It was either really early or really late. I wasn't sure which I would have preferred.

"Mostly," I said. "Thanks for...what you did."

She waved a hand. "It was my pleasure. I'm sure you'll return the favor one day."

I wasn't sure that I could, but if I could, I knew that I would. "Here's hoping I never have to. What the heck happened?"

"Your mother must have held on to a piece of you when you left. A hair or something similar. She bound herself to your dreams and, in so doing, tried to pull your soul from your body."

I don't know why I was expecting a more complicated response, but there it was. "Oh."

"I can assume she was going to pass your prophecy on to her other daughter."

Yeah, I thought, that sounded about right. "Well, what can we do to stop that from happening again?"

Marquessa seemed to think that over. "Dream magic is not something I know very well. I will have to call a few people, see what I can do. Perhaps I should have been doing that, anyway. It was prideful, mayhap even foolish of me, to think that I and my granddaughter, would be enough to handle this. Foolish to think that a child would be born fast enough that the Order would never know until it was too late."

If I had had it in me to be angry, I would have been, but I was too tired for that. "You know about the Order? What they wanted?"

She nodded. "I knew. That first night...when your mother appeared...I suspected, later...I knew."

A tinge of anger flickered through me. "Maybe next time don't keep it a secret."

She nodded. "You're right. I should have told you. For that, I am sorry."

See, I thought to my mom. *That's how you apologize. No excuses, no crap. Just a flat out 'I'm wrong.'*

"Who will you call?"

Marquessa sighed. "Whoever will listen. There are only so many witches, but I will call the ones I know, and they will call the ones they know."

"It sounds like an army." I meant it as a joke, but the solemn face she gave me told me this was probably not a laughing matter. "That's a fun expression."

"She attacked you, Lorena. That's an act of war if I ever heard one."

She swung suddenly to standing. "The first thing you can do is revitalize the wards in this place. Its occupant has been gone too long."

"Here I thought that you were going to send me back to the vampire house."

She gave me a knowing smile. "If I thought you would stay there, I jus' might."

She had a point there. I had absolutely no desire to stay at that place. While it had the kind of opulence that a lot of people might like to revel in, I couldn't help but feel a little overwhelmed there, though that might have more to do with the men than it had to do with my feelings on wealth. "Why do I get the feeling that you are leaving?"

She reached over and patted my cheek. "Many witches do not live where technology can touch. I'll have to travel a while. Be safe. Learn to protect yourself."

She stood up slowly and looked back over her shoulder. "Dreams are a scary place, Lorena, even without magic involved."

Her words made my skin tingle, and I wasn't sure why.

~~

Jenny had left me a note saying she'd be over when she got off of work. That I needed to rest. To stay indoors. I smirked. Was this what having a family was about? Not the trying to kill me so that a big fancy prophecy could work out how they wanted, but the caring about each other part? I hoped so. I liked that.

Rest, I thought. *I could do that.* I was a gamer and a nerd. Resting was something I knew how to do. I plopped myself down on the couch and pulled out some comics, re-read some DC to get into the mindset of being all powerful, and then decided it was time for video games. A couple hours later, I had died seven times and decided I might not be as great at this resting thing as I thought.

Marquessa was gathering a miniature army of witches. I had nearly had my soul sucked out. My dreams were no longer a safe place. And I was pretty sure I had seen Wei's eyes in my dreams. Ugh. Coming to my grandmother's was supposed to have made my life less complicated, not more so.

When it got dark, I made myself a sandwich. Someone, Jenny probably, had stocked my fridge with easy-to-make meals. I appreciated that. Complicated anything was just not what I wanted right now.

I had just taken my first bite of ham and swiss when I heard a cat meow. I blinked, suddenly remembering the sound of the cat in my dream. It had come right after the flash of eyes. I frowned at that. The feeling in the dream had been a good one, an empowering one. Besides, cats were cool. I set the sandwich down and did the most cliché thing in the world.

"Here, kitty kitty."

I felt a tiny tug of magic. Not much. No more than a spider web's worth of a tug. But when I looked up, a cat was sitting by my sandwich. At first glance, he (I was only guessing on the gender part) was sitting by my sandwich, sniffing regally at the bread. He was a gray tabby with a slender and long body and a tuft of white at his neck.

"Hello there."

He turned his eyes on mine, and I went still. That cat wasn't real. Okay, I felt like it was there, but it wasn't really real. It was, if I was guessing right, a ghost. It flickered just a little as I focused on it. Like a gif that didn't quite match its loop.

It meowed at me again and sniffed at my sandwich.

"Ghost cat," I said with a nod. "My life just gets weirder and weirder by the minute."

In the grand scheme of things, a ghost cat eyeing my dinner was not the weirdest thing that had happened to me recently. *Then again, I thought, if I was supposed to be a necromancer, maybe ghosts just showing up in my kitchen was a thing that was going to happen.* That was possible. Here's hoping they all looked like this cat.

It decided that it didn't want my dinner and flopped over on the counter between the piece of dividing paper from the cheese and the knife that I had used to spread the mayo on the bread. Its tail flicked, and it stretched out, offering me a surprisingly plump belly to touch. I wondered if I could. I reached out, and my fingers met fur, soft and full but a little cold to the touch.

It purred, and I felt a little better for it.

"Well, kitty," I said, plucking up my sandwich. "I'm gonna go read. Do you wanna join me?"

It eyed me for a moment. I shrugged, deciding that if it wanted to follow me, it would. I kinda liked the idea of having a ghost cat friend.

When I got back to my grandmother's room, it was already there.

"I guess that's a yes. You gonna guard me as I get better? Because I'm down for that."

I plopped down, and it curled up on the pillow next to me, closing its eyes and stretching out its toes. I watched the ghost for a moment. Okay, right that moment, I wasn't positive that it was a ghost, but I was pretty sure, at least ninety-eight percent. The colors weren't quite right. I mean, he, and I were pretty sure he was a he, had the gray, white, and black colors of a tabby. The colors, however, were muted, as if the intensity had been turned down.

The feline seemed to breathe too. As I ate the first few bites of my sandwich, I watched the steady rise and fall of its middle, but I was almost positive that it wasn't alive. Not just because it had managed to teleport from the kitchen to the bedroom, but because of my own magical skill. The presence of the cat was a weight in my mind, and a comforting one at that. It stretched again, and the collar around its neck twinkled.

I reached out and turned the little name tag until I could read what was written there. Maahes, the letters spelled. I frowned. That was an odd name. But the address below was familiar. It was my grandmother's address. Had this, once upon a time, been my grandmother's cat? Maybe. It would explain why it was hanging around here. I gave the feline's chin a scratch. It purred in response, and I decided I now had a ghost friend. I queued up a novel on an app on my smart phone. I was just getting to the good part when I heard a knock on my grandmother's door.

My heart hammered inside of my chest. The cat didn't budge. So much for a guard pet. There was a part of me that wanted nothing more than to pull the blankets up to my chin and pretend like I wasn't there. I shook, and sweat appeared on my skin. I went from being relaxed to being afraid for my life in two point three seconds.

"Lorena?"

It was Wei's voice. I didn't relax exactly, but I felt a little less afraid for my life.

"Wei?" I asked. I had to ask it twice because the first time it came out as a choked whisper. "What are you doing here?"

"I. wanted to speak with you."

It was quite nearly a speech as far as Wei was concerned, no matter how bluntly he said it. I opened the door, and there he stood.

Wei was never going to have Alan's elegance, or Dmitri's fiery charisma, but he had his own kind of beauty, and I had to admit that

I was drawn to it. His long sheet of pitch black hair was pulled into a thick braid. It hung over one shoulder, making a line of black over the sapphire blue of the shirt he wore. I was almost positive it was made of silk; it had that particular sheen. His dark slacks had a quality to them, the kind that whispered wealth rather than screamed it the way some wealthy people's clothes did. Not that I had a lot of experience with the high class, but, thanks to Jenny, I was learning more about fashion.

"What did you want to talk about?" I asked, leaning against the door frame. I should have told him to go away, but I couldn't. In the time that I had known Wei, he had never come to me for anything, and I was curious about what he had to say.

"May I come in?" he asked.

I shrugged and stepped back. "Sure. Come on in. Meet the ghost cat?"

He frowned. "Ghost cat?"

Maahes was sitting on the arm of my grandmother's floral easy chair. His bright eyes blinked solemnly as Wei walked into the living room. For a moment, I wondered whether or not Wei could even see the cat, and then he held out one hand towards the feline. The cat sniffed and then bumped his head against Wei's fingers.

"You make interesting friends."

I smirked. "More and more every day." I sat down on the couch. Maahes jumped down and sauntered over to me. "What did you want to talk about?"

He stood there quietly for a moment. The sun, just barely set, was still letting off just enough sunlight that shadows played across his handsome features. He was looking down, rather than at me.

"I wanted to apologize."

Wow, I thought to myself, everyone just wanted to apologize to me today: my mother, Marquessa, and now Wei. Must be some kind of planetary alignment thing. "Take a number."

"What?"

I shook my head. "Bad joke, never mind. What did you want to apologize for?"

"For...what happened...between us."

Jeez. If this was how Wei said he was sorry for something, it was going to take forever to get through.

"For which part?" I asked. "For the wild make out session? For you eyeballing my throat like it was a tasty, tasty treat? Or for running away from me and leaving me with a throbbing case of blue-ovaries?"

He jerked his head up. "Blue...ovaries?"

I shrugged. "I figure if guys can say they get blue balls without there being any scientific evidence to back it up, I can claim blue ovaries. I mean, I don't know if you have a clear memory of what happened in that big old bed, but it was getting pretty hot and heavy. Then, you left me high and dry. Well...okay...not exactly dry, but-"

He made a sound that was somewhere between a snort of surprise and a choked laugh. It was an impressive sound.

"You baffle me."

I shrugged. "I bet you say that to all the girls."

He sighed and finally took a seat. "I want to explain my actions."

"I could handle an explanation."

Rather than launch into that, he sat there in the ever-growing darkness. His hands were flat on the arm rests; I could see bits of the flower design through his broad fingers. For a moment, just a moment, all I could do was remember how good his hands had felt. The way he had kissed. The way I had arched to his hand. I shivered.

"Lorena."

"Yes?"

"Whatever you are thinking about...please stop."

I blushed. Well, that answered the question about how good a vampire's senses were. I didn't bother to reach for a light. I had no desire to show him the depth of the blush on my cheeks.

"Sorry."

"It's...fine."

Another long lapse of silence.

"So, before I begin to think lecherous thoughts and embarrass us any further, how about you tell me what happened?"

He blew out a long breath. "I was married once."

I blinked. I wasn't sure what I had expected to hear from him, but that certainly hadn't been it. "Oh." I fought a tinge of unexpected jealousy that cropped up inside me. "What happened?"

He splayed his fingers further apart, revealing more of the pattern. "Marriages were different when I was alive. My bride was chosen for me."

"An arranged marriage?" I asked. I didn't know that they had done that in China. Then again, I was assuming he was Chinese. Shame on me.

He shook his head. "Not exactly. It was not as if I would have no say in who I married. But our parents were very involved in the match. After all, this woman would be the vessel of their legacy, their continued honor. It was very important that she be everything that they desired for me."

"What about love?" I asked, knowing how naive it sounded.

His smile was bitter. "Love was...not important. But the process was complicated: who her parents were, who mine were, when we were born, what skills we both had, whether or not the relationship might bear a son. I do not wish to bore you with the details, but my parents chose a girl that I... did not enjoy."

I drew Maahes into my lap, desperate for something to do with my hands. "I'm sorry." I said it quietly. I don't think he heard me.

"Her name was Jiaya. She was pretty enough, I suppose, and polite enough. But she had no mind of her own. I have always been partial to a woman who speaks her mind." His eyes glanced up to meet mine. I didn't need to say the obvious, but I found myself smiling at him anyway.

"Yes. But she was very quiet. Very meek. It was not some great fault, but I made it into one. I slowly began to hate everything that she said. We would sit for long hours, and she would do her best to try to please me with conversation, but...but I did not like her very much. I am ashamed to admit that I did not treat her well. She tried. She tried very hard to win my affection, even my attention, and I had already decided that she could never have it. My own stubbornness trapped us in an unhappy union."

I could see it, I realized. I could see this little bride with a shy smile and bright eyes looking at Wei, so handsome and proud, and thinking that she had won the bridal lottery, only to be very disappointed because her handsome husband was also cold. I could also see Wei becoming more and more stubborn about her. Their parents had not chosen well.

"Then what?"

"She asked me to give her a child."

I didn't hold my breath, but it was a near thing. "Oh."

"She begged. She said if I could not bring myself to care for her, she would not seek it, but would I please give her a son to love and who might love her in return. She would even settle for a daughter, which, in those feudal days, was a great sacrifice. Just something to give her heart to. I hated her for asking me, but I could not bring myself to deny her. I... did my best..." he said. His own blush turned his cheeks a rosy bronze. "It was not a comfortable thing for either of us, but there was a child. A son. She was so proud. To be honest, I was proud too. We named him Gui and, like all parents, had great expectations of him."

"It sounds like everything was happy."

His hand clenched. "It should have been. It might have been. I don't know. Her happiness did not last. She became very...sad. Very distant. She did not want to feed the child. She alternated between wanting to love him and hating herself for being a terrible mother. I was, I admit, confused."

I swallowed. Postpartum depression was not a new thing, and it wasn't just something that happened in America. I knew that, logically, but imagining some ancient girl in feudal China going through it boggled my mind. "It happens."

He nodded. "I know. At least, I know that now. I didn't then. I just...I hated her more. Here was this child we created, and she wanted less and less to do with him every day. I got mad at her. I made things worse."

I wasn't sure that I wanted to hear the end of this story. It could not be going anywhere good. I continued to pet the cat, though it wasn't really doing any good for my growing anxiety.

"I had to leave the home for several days in order to take an examination. I had hoped to do well in order to make sure that my son might have a better life. It felt so good to be out of the home, away from Jaiya. I lingered. I met a widow who liked to speak her mind. I enjoyed her company. I should have gone back immediately. I never took the widow to bed, but I wished to. Then, I received a letter. It was from my mother. She told me that I must return home immediately. I knew; even before I returned, I knew what had happened. My bride had drowned our son."

"Oh my god."

He went very quiet. "She was so angry at me. So wild. She blamed me. She snapped at me and yelled at me and snarled at me. She was like some great tiger lashing out. It was the first time I had ever heard her speak her mind. She asked me how I could have expected her to love something that had come from a man as cold and angry as I was."

My heart sank all the way to my knees. I didn't like that Jaiya had said that. It left a bad taste in my mouth. You didn't have to love a father to love the kid...though it did help some things. "I'm so sorry, Wei."

"She waited just long enough to know that I had heard her words, and then she took a blade to her own throat."

"Oh my god."

He nodded. "Yes. I left my home after that. My parents had another son, young but warmer of heart. I traveled a great deal. Eventually, I met Vlad," he said with a note of finality.

"Wei, I'm so sorry that you went through that. It's...well, it sucks."

"It did. But I hope it explains some things to you."

I blinked at that. "Explains...what?"

He turned those liquid dark eyes on me, and they were filled with that cool superiority that I had grown to know so well. "Lorena, laying with you might...is expected...to create a child. How can I give another woman who does not love me that burden?"

Jesus. I took a deep breath and set the purring cat aside. Rather than just flop over or give me a sneer like a normal cat might have done, it disappeared. I hoped it wouldn't stay gone, but it was not my biggest concern now. I walked over to Wei, and then knelt in front of him, using a leftover pillow to cushion my knees.

"Wei, let's be honest here."

He eyed me warily. "About?"

"You care about me."

I wasn't willing to say that he loved me, but I was pretty sure that he did. Wei was a vampire. I was a necromancer. He might be able to sense when I was feeling all needy for his body, but I could sense what he was feeling too. He liked me a lot more than he was willing to admit.

"Lorena-"

"You care about me," I said, cutting him neatly off, "and I care about you. I won't call what I feel love. It's not that. Not yet. But I care about you. I like your stubbornness. I like your rare smiles. And, dear god, I really liked how it felt when you put your hands all over me." I ran my hands up his thighs.

He made a sound. "Lorena!" He grabbed my wrists hard between his own.

"What?" I demanded as he pulled me back from his body.

"Do not pretend to feel what you don't."

"Who the heck says I'm pretending?" I demanded.

He gave me an angry look. If it had been Dmitri, I might have been afraid to see that simmering anger, but it wasn't. Wei I trusted to keep control of his emotions, even when those emotions raged. That was a pretty big thing as far as I was concerned.

"What of Alan?"

"Alan is in love with Dmitri, and even if he weren't, he's a little flamboyant for my personal tastes."

"Dmitri?"

I shook my head once. "Weirdly enough, the fear of him one day losing control and beasting out on me does not endear him to me."

"Zane?"

"Mr. Enigma?" I asked. "We've barely exchanged three words to one another. Why would I have feelings for him?"

Wei snarled at me. I jerked my hands out of his grasp. "I get that you have baggage because your first wife didn't handle you well, but that doesn't mean that you aren't able to be loved."

He frowned at me. "You don't love me. You said so."

I glared at him. "You haven't actually given me a chance. But even with that being said...everything that I have learned, I have loved. Even knowing about your son and your ex. Even knowing how stupidly stubborn you can be. How you like to hide all of your feelings behind this mask of cool distance. If you gave me half a chance, Wei, I would absolutely love you, but you are too damn afraid to accept that."

I felt angry, and I didn't even know why. I hadn't realized just how deep my feelings for the taciturn vampire went until right this moment. Was I crazy for feeling this way? Probably a little. But here I was.

He tried to step away, but I grabbed his wrist. He used some fancy martial arts move to pull away from me, but I was better than that. Up until this week, I had been training with Wei three nights a week; I knew how to read his movements. I stepped up with him, and the next thing I knew, we were sparring. His heart wasn't in it though. I might be a good learner, but I only had a month under my belt. He had a few centuries and super human speed, but my magic gave me insight into his motions.

It still wasn't enough. I stumbled back and plopped down on the floor, but I grabbed his silken shirt and carried him with me. We rolled on the ground, and I straddled his hips. I felt him beneath me and reveled in the fact that he was, at the very least, half interested in being pinned beneath me. I ground myself against him, and he made a bestial sound in response.

"Lorena!"

"Wei," I groaned, lowering my mouth to his. There was nothing light or gentle about this kiss. This was full of tongue and teeth and fire. I wanted him; I wanted him so badly that I burned for it.

His hands were quick as they tugged at my clothes, and all I wanted him to do was take me back to the bedroom. Heck, I was pretty much okay with just making it back to the couch. The floor, with its numerous scattered pillows, would have been a pretty good choice too, as far as my quickly waking libido was concerned.

His hands folded over my hips and hauled me closer to him. I could feel how much he wanted me. I was drowning in it, and I was so totally okay with that. I was ready, oh so ready.

And then Wei froze.

I think I said "no," but it might have been more of a growl. Scratch that. It was definitely more of a growl. He gripped my hands and held them still, and it was then that I heard it: the sound of a car pulling into the drive way. I blinked, wondering who or what could possibly be interrupting this moment. Then, I heard the sound of Jenny's laugh and remembered that she was supposed to be coming over.

"Jenny," I told him.

He put a full foot of distance between us, readjusting his silk shirt so that it didn't look like I had yanked it out of his pants.

"You should choose Zane," he said flatly.

I blinked. "Wait, what?"

"Zane will be a good father to your child, and a good partner to you. He is strong and he is capable."

I wanted to argue with him, but then he turned into smoke. One moment, he was there, beautiful and haughty and closed off from me. The next, he was a wisp of gray mist fleeing from my grandmother's house.

"Now, wait a minute!" I shouted, just as Jenny walked through the door, a wide-eyed Reikah in her wake.

"What's wrong?" Jenny asked, holding up several grease-laden bags of burgers and fries. "What happened?"

Reikah looked over her shoulder, her nose wrinkling prettily. "Vampire."

Jenny raised her brow and took stock of my appearance. I could only imagine what she saw. My hair was mussed, and not just from sleep. My pajamas weren't quite sitting right on my hips, and there was a clear flush on my cheeks.

"Did you mate the vampire?" Reikah wanted to know.

"Rude," Jenny said over her shoulder, "but did you?"

I slapped my palms over my face and flopped down into the chair that Wei had been sitting in before everything had gotten all handsy. "No... looks like it's blue ovaries again."

Jenny made a sound of sympathy and patted my shoulder. "Would some burgers and milkshakes help?"

I thought it over. While I would definitely prefer sinking my teeth into Wei right this moment, a burger was a close second.

"Alright."

"I do not eat meat," Reikah said.

Jenny shot her a look. "Why didn't you tell me before now?"

"I did not know that I was going to be invited to dine with you. I believed I was here to teach wizardry. We should practice first," Reikah said. "It is the cusp of the later darkness, a good time to do magic."

Jenny rolled her eyes. "Any time is a good time for magic, but these fries, which aren't meat, will get cold, and weirdos are the only ones who like cold fries."

Reikah lifted her nose into the air. "Simply because you choose to practice magic with no sense of discipline does not mean that any time is a good time for magic. The day is separated into four parts. Dawn, noon, dusk, and midnight. The time between dusk and midnight is when you should begin casting spells for understanding and wisdom. I believe that our mutual friend could benefit from wisdom, do you not agree?"

I thought 'friend' was pushing it. I didn't dislike Reikah, and I was very aware that I probably owed her my life, which was a bond all on its own. But friend was someone that you could call whenever you needed to vent about life, and I'd never had the itch to tell Reikah about the deeper inner workings of being me.

"That's bull," Jenny said, plopping the bags onto the small kitchen table. "The whole idea that the time of day and the day of the week influence your magic is a bunch of superstition."

Reikah lifted one black brow. "It amuses me that a mountain witch attempts to lecture me on superstition."

Jenny's eyes took on a fire I had never seen before. "Sweetie, this mountain witch could kick your butt no matter the time of the day or the day of the week."

"Burgers," I said, reaching for the bags. "We are going to have burgers now. Then, you are going to explain what it is I am supposed to be getting wise about. Okay?"

The two women eyed one another for a long moment.

"Buuurgers," I coaxed. I really hoped it worked. "Come on. I can tell you about my new ghost friend while we are at it."

That got their attention. Jenny looked intrigued. Reikah looked suspicious.

"What ghost friend?"

"He's a cat. A gray tabby. The collar around his neck says Maahes."

Jenny's lips, painted a bright rosy bronze, spread into a big smile. "Awww, I had hoped he was around. Where is he?"

I shrugged and plopped down in one of the dining chairs. The other two girls followed suit, and I began to dish out burgers and fries to everyone. "I dunno. He decided to be discrete and disappeared not too long before Wei got to second base with me."

"Who is Maahes?" Reikah asked, offering a large chocolate shake to each of us.

I opened three ketchup packets and made a mountain to dip my fries in. "Well, after a quick look on Google, I can tell you that Maahes is an Egyptian god of war and protection, often depicted as a cat or a lion."

"He was Miz Loretta's cat, Lorena's grandma. He was around for forever, it seemed like. Long-bodied, great markings around the eyes. Good cat."

I felt a little twinge in my chest. "He was my grandmother's?" I had known that, or rather, I had guessed it. But hearing it come out of Jenny's mouth was a shock to my system.

I had never met my grandmother, but everywhere I turned, she had affected my life. When I was born, she had been the one to speak the prophecy, saying that the child that I gave birth to, via the blood of a son of Vlad, would bring magic back into the world. Magic, as I had learned, had slowly been dying away.

There were a lot of theories about why, but the most popular was that the ley lines, invisible highways of magic that wrapped around the world, were broken. How my offspring was supposed to go about fixing that, I hadn't the foggiest idea, but I was pretty cool with the idea of magic being a thing. Apparently, dragons might come back. I like dragons...well, in theory, I like dragons.

My grandmother, prophetess and witch of the Virginia Appalachians, had wanted to raise me. My father, whose exact reasons for taking me away were still a mystery to me, had decided to get me as far away from my grandmother as he could. Then again, I thought as I dipped one fry into a blob of ketchup, maybe he had just been trying to get me away from my creepy cultist mother. Jeez. I still don't know how those two had hooked up. Then again, does anyone ever really know why their parents are, or were, an item?

"All witches should have a companion," Reikah said, interrupting my thoughts.

"Do you?" I asked.

She pushed her nose into the air, a neat trick since she was already looking down her nose at us. "I am not a witch. I am an adept of the Order of-"

I rolled my eyes. "Yes, yes, I know, sacred hermit or whatever. So, what, adepts don't have animal companions?"

She sniffed as if I had said something bad. "It is...not our way."

"What is your way?" Jenny asked.

"We are practitioners of sorcery, not witchcraft. Ours is a finely-honed talent."

I sighed; I could already see Jenny's eyes flickering with emotion. I did not have it in me to referee a fight about the ins and outs of magic, especially since I really didn't see a huge difference between the two schools of thought here. "Okay, so, why are you here? I mean, I don't mean to sound crabby, but I wasn't expecting you."

Reikah lifted her brow again. "Indeed. Considering the state we found you in, you were not expecting anyone."

Jenny snorted a laugh, and I felt my cheeks go from their natural pink to candy apple red. I attempted several explanations before I gave up and took a bite from my burger. "I don't know if I am in love with the vampire, but I am in serious and deep lust."

Jenny shrugged, doing her best to look unruffled. "There ain't nothing wrong with some good old-fashioned lust."

Reikah responded, saying "Lust will distract. It is better to choose a male whom you trust to protect you."

CHAPTER SIX

As the three of us practiced magic, Reikah's words remained on my mind. I knew by the way that she had said them that she meant them. *Maybe she was right*, I thought. Maybe it was impossible to choose a guy for love under these circumstances. Love, as far as I was concerned, was supposed to happen naturally, like a flower blooming. I couldn't just go from one thing to the next and hope to be in love.

But, as Alan was fond of telling me, you didn't have to be in love to have a child. People got knocked up every day without feeling anything for the person who helped make that life.

"You are thinking long thoughts," Reikah said. Her eyes were narrowed with disappointment. "You need to concentrate."

I frowned down at the paper in front of me. It was black and lineless. Next to that was a green colored pencil. I had done my best to draw a perfect circle in the very center of the paper, but it looked more like a football, and I was pretty sure it was nowhere near the center.

"I don't understand why I need to learn this," I said, poking at the center of the circle.

"There is no one reason, but if you'd like, I can name several."

Reikah sat back on her heels, managing to make it look graceful. Jenny had gone home to get sleep for the night, since she and a couple of her relatives were running the shop while her grandmother, Marquessa, was off gathering an army. I hadn't realized until Jenny was walking out the door that Reikah had planned on staying the night with me. I quickly learned that it was a more permanent arrangement. After all she had said, I couldn't expect her to live under the roof of vampires without me there.

I had no clue what I had to do with anything, but it was clear that she wasn't comfortable going back to the mansion. Fine. Whatever. She could try to teach me her form of magic if she really wanted to. Spoiler alert, she totally wanted to.

Which is why we were sitting in the very center of my grandmother's house. Not just from the northern point to the southern point, but from east to west as well. Apparently, when it came to wizardry, which was different from and superior to witchcraft in all ways, according to Reikah, where you were mattered as much as when you were and how you were. Oh, goody.

"Go ahead," I told her.

"The first and most logical reason for you to learn the basics of wizardry is that your main and most common enemy will be The Order itself. It will do you a great deal of good to understand how they operate and what they believe."

Okay, that was fair. "But why can't I just hear it from you? You could, you know, just tell me."

She gave me that look that told me I was being dumb again. I was not fond of that look, and Reikah seemed to perpetually think that I was inferior to her grand magical ways. It was probably true, but she didn't need to rub it in.

"Because it is not really learning. I could lecture you, yes, but the mind does not really understand something until you learn to do it with your own hands."

I sighed and looked down at my pitiful excuse for a circle. "Okay, but my hands don't seem to be learning much."

"Do you expect to be perfect the first time you try? Mine is not as good as it should be, but you do not see me crying about it, do you?"

I glanced at the piece of paper sitting in front of her. If her circle wasn't perfect, I couldn't tell. "Yeah, okay."

She sighed and held up the paper, and proceeded to fold it in half, and then in half again. When she opened it back up, I could see that the circle she had drawn, also in green, wasn't in the exact middle, but just barely.

"That looks pretty damn good," I said.

She sighed and laid it down again. "It would barely work, but it will have to do."

"If you say so. Okay, we both have our circles, now what?"

"A circle...if you want to call what you drew a circle...is the beginning of all magic. Magic, you have to understand, is not unlike water; it wishes to move, to flow, to fill an available space. That circle creates a space for it to go."

I nodded; that made sense. "And magic cares that the circle is perfect?"

"Magic is not alive, not like you or I. It is an energy, and while it will fill any offered circle, provided that it is properly called, a lopsided circle will cause the magic to fill in unevenly, and that can, in many situations, cause problems."

I held up my excellent attempt at a football doodle. "So, I should try again, shouldn't I?"

She shrugged her shoulders. "I assumed that you wished to go about magic with the same flippant attitude of your friend."

That got my hackles up. "Watch how you talk about Jenny. She's a good person."

Reikah kept her eyes on her paper. "She may have the best of intentions, but her actions do absolutely nothing to help heal the wounds of the world."

Now there was a term that I hadn't heard. "Wait, what wounds? What are you talking about?"

She narrowed her eyes at me. "You don't know?"

"Would I ask if I knew? I mean, do I strike you as that kind of girl?"

She seemed to take the question far more seriously than I meant it. "I don't know," she finally answered. "I know you only as a woman who wishes to fulfill destiny."

"Well," I said, reaching for another piece of construction paper from a massive pile that I had found in my grandmother's closet, "I am not the kind of girl who would waste time asking dumb questions. There are far better ways to waste my time."

"I do not know why anyone would like to waste time at all."

I had to chuckle at that. "Remind me to introduce you to my PlayStation when we are done here. But that being said, what the heck are the wounds of the world?"

"The places where magic no longer flows," she told me.

"Okay, I know something about that. There are ley lines that don't have magic going where it ought to, like broken highways."

She gave me a long look. "And? Why do you think they are that way?"

It was my turn to raise my brow at her. "I think the better question here is why you think that they are that way. You are, after all, supposed to be teaching me how the Order thinks."

She folded her hands in her lap in a prim fashion and settled down to the ground. "Because, many years ago, magic was a wild thing. It did whatever it wanted, whenever it wanted, at the hands of a person who knew even the most basic understanding of the craft. It was like a string pulled too tight between too many hands over and over again. It has frayed, and in many places snapped."

"I see," I said. I had heard a version of this before, similar enough that I was willing to believe most of it. "So, you think that by putting magic back into the world, we are going to go through the same thing again?"

She shook her head. "I don't. It is impossible to say what may happen again. Just because it happened before does not mean that it will happen that way again. Human beings, and society at large, while prone to certain patterns, are, in essence, chaotic."

I frowned. "You talk like a Jane Austen novel sometimes, you know that?"

She smiled. It was a good smile. "I am fond of her novels."

"What?" I asked, legitimately shocked. "Miss precise lady likes romance novels?"

She shrugged. "Romance novels in a setting where there are rules and structure, yes."

Okay, that made more sense. I thought of Jenny now, and the way that she had looked when she talked about Reikah. It didn't quite match up to the way she looked when she was talking to Reikah, but that didn't mean that there wasn't any hope. If Austen taught me anything, it was that two stubborn people with a difference in opinion could fall in love. "Is that all you want in a relationship? Rules and structure?"

"I do not know what that has to do with anything."

I shrugged, doing my best to appear nonchalant. "We are friends, right?"

She gave me a look. "We...are."

"Jeez, you don't need to say that as if I were pulling out your teeth."

"You are not pulling out my teeth, but you are treading into uncomfortable conversation." Her eyes stayed fixed firmly on the black paper in front of her. I hadn't known Reikah for very long at all, just a couple of days really; I was in no way an expert, but I was pretty sure that she was very uncomfortable.

I frowned. "I'm sorry." I meant it.

She sighed. "It is not your fault. People are naturally curious." She used her long fingers to flatten out her recently folded paper. "I have never been in a relationship; I have never had any desire to be. I do not know how I would handle it, or if it is even something that I want."

I had heard of people who were asexual or aromantic before, but I had to admit that it wasn't something I really understood. As far as I could tell, they were just people who didn't experience attraction. I, personally, couldn't picture that, but just because I didn't know what it would be like didn't mean that it wasn't a real thing.

"It's no big deal," I finally said. "If you don't want a romance, you don't have to have one. There is nothing wrong with you if you don't."

She gave me another one of those Jon Snow looks, the one where I felt like I knew nothing. "How can you possibly believe that?"

I shrugged again, picking up the green colored pencil. Then, I set it down and folded my paper into quarters and opened it up again. I wished I had some kind of protractor or something, but my grandmother did not seem to be the kind of woman who would have had one around.

"Why shouldn't I?"

"I just told you I enjoy Austen's books."

I snorted. "Let me get this straight. You think because you like a romance novelist, or a person who enjoys romance in general, that you must want to be in a romantic relationship? For someone claiming to be logical, that's a pretty weird point of view."

"Why?" she demanded.

"I like murder mysteries, but I don't want to go kill someone and lead police officers on a wild goose chase. I play lots of video games, but I don't want to live all of those stories. Some of them, sure, but not all of them. You don't have to always want a romantic partner. It's fine if you don't."

"They say that sex and love are some of the core desires of being human." This time, she did look at me. Her eyes were filled with an emotion I could not understand.

Jesus, I was not the best person to be having this conversation with. I'd never doubted my identity, sexual or otherwise. Sure, I'd been out on a date with another girl, but at the end of the day, I considered myself to be straight, mostly. Here was this girl who I hadn't even known for a full seventy-two hours, who had spent her time with a group that had all the earmarks of a magical cult, complete with creepy leader, and she was telling me that she was, at the very least, confused about herself. Crap. I did not know how to deal with this.

On top of that, I was feeling sorry for Jenny. Jenny, who knew who and what she was but lived in a place where there were not a whole lot of options to express herself. I had officially found myself in a rock meets hard place situation. I could suggest to Reikah that she ought to explore, try things, whatever. Maybe arrange things so that she ended up going out with Jenny...but that seemed like a crappy thing to do.

No, I decided, I hadn't. I loved Jenny, but that didn't mean I had to push Reikah to do absolutely anything that she wasn't comfortable with.

"Yeah, and a hundred years ago," I continued, " we didn't think that women could enjoy sex. Thirty years ago, we thought anyone who wasn't totally and completely straight was suffering from a mental illness. I mean, what we know about humanity changes from one span of years to the next. You are a human being; you need to know what that means to you."

She gave me a long look. "Perhaps you aren't as stupid as I thought you were."

"Cool. I'll take that as a compliment. Now, teach me your super strict magical system before I take back all the nice things I might say about you."

"How kind of you. That circle is far less imperfect."

"See, now you are getting better at this complimenting thing."

She didn't quite smile, but it was close.

~~

My first attempt at wizardry can only be described as a failure of nearly epic proportions. I attempted, via careful lines and confusing symbols, to summon the element of air. I am proud to say that I succeeded. A very small tornado had a short lifespan inside of my grandmother's living room. It was terrifying and neat all at the same time. When Reikah used her fancy skills to rip up my paper and thus banish the element, she decided that I needed more practice, but that that night wasn't the best time.

I was tired, and decided that she was absolutely right.

Reikah took up residence on my couch, and if I was being completely honest, I was kind of happy to have her there. I didn't know her well, but I trusted her just enough to think that if something terrible happened when I was sleeping, she'd do something about it.

I made my way back to my grandmother's bedroom. No, I thought, it was my bedroom. I was sleeping here now. The bed couldn't belong to a dead woman, no matter how strong her presence might have been in life, and I was one hundred percent certain that she had been a powerful person in life.

When I walked in, there was Maahes, curled up on one of the pillows like a feline prince. The pillow did not notice the weight; there was no divot beneath his body, but I was happy that he was there too. I grabbed a change of pajamas and went to take a shower, wondering if it was a good thing or a bad thing to spend an entire day wearing pajamas...I was going to go with good. Pajamas were awesome.

I picked up my phone, played a few games, and then switched to a novel. When I thought about getting up and investigating my grandmother's closet, I realized I was putting off going to sleep. It didn't take a therapist to understand why. Even my brain, lacking in college education, knew that I just didn't want another crazy dream. I'd had pretty much enough of those.

I dragged my hand down my face and plopped back against my pillow. Maahes stretched his feet out until the tips of one paw brushed my cheek. It made me smile, short-lived as it was. I'd never had a cat; I'd never had a pet at all. My father had moved me around too much. He said it would be too difficult with his job.

With the kind of courage that you can only get at one-thirty in the morning, I picked up my phone. I very nearly called my father, but the hour was not quite late enough for that kind of courage. Instead, I sent a text.

"How much of this prophecy stuff do you believe? Is my mother crazy? Why did we travel all over the country?"

There, I thought, hitting send, that was good enough. Right. Sure.

I plopped the phone down, not really expecting to get an answer this late. Instead, I crawled out of bed and started looking around my grandmother's bedroom. No, I had to tell myself for the umpteenth time, *my* bedroom. Everything here was mine. The books on magic, the crystals cluttering the dishes, the simple wooden furniture. They were mine. They just didn't feel like it.

I had never owned all that much before. Like I said, I moved around a lot. For most of my life, a couple of boxes of books, games, and comics were all that I had really treasured. I'd never had a lot of clothes. I couldn't say that we were poor; we weren't, but we never had all that much either.

I opened the top dresser drawer. Mostly undergarments. I probably wasn't going to keep those. It was a little weird to keep my grandmother's bras. The second drawer was t-shirts, comfortable-looking and well taken care of. My grandmother and I shared a love of comfortable clothing in common, I discovered as I found that she had more sweatpants than she had jeans or slacks. She did, however, own a lot of bohemian clothes. I might go through those and keep some of them. I didn't want to get rid of her completely.

I went to the closet and rooted around in there for a while. There were shoes, not in my size, and some nicer dresses. Cute ones, but nothing that I'd wear. Behind all of that, in what looked like an old-fashioned hat box, I found a set of journals.

Jackpot, I thought as I pulled them into my lap. They were the epitome of variety; some of the journals were fancy, leather-bound and hand-stitched, and some were cheap dollar store composition books, but all of them were filled from front to back with the familiar scrawl of my grandmother's handwriting.

They started when she was sixteen. I had to be careful turning the brittle and yellowed pages of those earliest days, but as I read, I realized that, in a weird and distant way, I was meeting my grandmother.

July 15th, 1961

Today is my birthday, and my Great Aunt Sandra decided that a journal was a good enough gift for a young witch. I suppose it is. It is not the Buick that I had hoped for, but then again, it was probably foolish of me to ask for a car when daddy is still sending money back from the mines. I don't much like him working like he does. Aren't momma and I witches? Shouldn't we be able to provide? According to momma, we can't use our skills that way, but I don't know why not. Plenty of people would pay to learn the future. Why can't I tell them for money what I learn for free?

Daddy sent me a card with enough money to buy cloth for a dress. He asked that I wear it when he comes back at the end of summer. I'll ask Marquessa to go with me.

Maybe I'll wear it when Jake Quinn asks me out on that date he's trying to talk himself into. He's a good boy, and I've already seen that we will get married. He won't be a coal miner. I've seen that much. It'll be good enough for me.

July 27th, 1961

I bought a pink fabric. Marquessa says it'll look great on me. She ought to know. She looks great in everything. Then again, her sister is a fabric witch; she can make anything look good. I'd ask her to help me make my dress, but I don't think she likes me. That's okay. Seers make people uncomfortable. They think we know everything.

Momma will help me sew the dress. I wonder what is taking Jake so long to get around to asking me out. See, prophets don't know everything.

August 7th, 1961

Apparently, Jake has been distracted my Missy Mortin. What kind of name is Missy, anyway? A foolish one, that's what. It's alright. I won't hold it against Jake. He's just a boy, after all, and the idea of being in love with a witch makes him nervous. Not that he believes in witches.

Then again, why should I wait? Just because I know he'll be the man I marry; does that mean I shouldn't have a beau or two in the meantime? Just because I know it won't last, does that mean I shouldn't try at all?

August 19th, 1961

Daddy will be home before school starts up again. I saw it last night in my dreams. How do I tell momma it's because he lost his job, not because he got the time to come back and see us? Maybe I shouldn't tell her at all. I can pretend like I don't know. It'll be okay. It has to be okay.

August 31st, 1961

Daddy is home. Momma is mad at me that I didn't warn her about the job loss. She said she could have prepared. Prepared for what? Prepared how? I didn't see this years ago; I saw it two weeks ago. She didn't care to hear it. She said my gift was special. That I ought to be proud of what I could see, good or bad.

What would she know?

I had never thought about what it would be like to be a Seer. I closed the old journal and let it fall into my lap. Almost all of those early entries talked about how her seeing visions complicated things. If she knew who she was going to marry, should she bother with other romances in the meantime? If she had seen her father's layoff, should she tell her mother?

I found myself wondering if it was easier to be the prophecy teller or the one who the prophecy was about.

With that thought swimming in my head, I laid back on the floor. I stared up at the ceiling and placed a hand just beneath my belly button. My prophecy wasn't just about me though, was it? It was about me and the child I was going to have. What if that kid had no desire to bring magic into the word? Not everyone was like me, desperate to see all the fantastic things that I had daydreamed about.

Stack on top of that, the fact that I had no idea how the child was supposed to do this great task...talk about pressure.

A striped feline head peeped out over the edge of the bed. It opened its mouth and gave a soft meow. It didn't sound real. It was a meow, but it had a strange echo in it, as if I were listening to the sound in a bathroom.

I remembered the cat-like meow in my dream and wondered if there was some kind of connection.

Then, I thought about the eyes in the dream. At first, I'd thought they were Wei's, dark and luminous. But maybe they weren't. Just because I saw the eyes didn't mean that they were Wei's. They could have been anyone's, considering the moment. Maybe I just wanted them to be his.

This would be a whole lot easier, I thought, if a prophecy wasn't involved. I could just fall in love with whoever and go off to live my life like everyone else did. But no, here I was at two in the morning wondering about my late grandmother, the child I wasn't even close to having, and everyone involved.

The light from my phone caught my attention. I slid back into the bed, expecting one of the vampires to have sent me a message about coming home. Instead, it was from my father. I hesitated before opening it. I had asked some really heavy questions, and I wasn't entirely sure that I wanted the answers anymore.

Screw it, I thought, and swept my thumb across the screen to get the text.

"I'm sorry."

That's it. That's all. I frowned down at the phone face.

My dad didn't apologize all that often. He said that apologies meant you thought you did something wrong and he rarely did. Yeah, that was my dad alright, the son of a witch. The only time he ever really said he was sorry was when we had to move from one place to another, just as I was beginning to settle down. Ugh.

"Yeah," I said, a wealth of bitterness exploding from my lips. "I'll just bet you are."

I tossed down the phone and shook my head. The screen lit up again. Angry curiosity had me looking at it. Unknown sender. The text was similar to the other one I had received. Just a bunch of weird symbols. In a fit of disgust, I tossed the phone.

"Screw you, unknown sender; I've got too much going on to help you out."

I crawled back into bed, pulled my blankets up to my chin, and fell asleep.

CHAPTER SEVEN

Winter in Appalachia was no joke. The autumn had been warm enough, light enough. It had been gentle breezes and cool, clear nights. Winter was hard. The temperature dropped to twenty degrees as the middle of December approached. I had spent the past few weeks cleaning up my house, reading my grandmother's journals, learning magic, and, after some deliberation, letting the vampires visit from time to time.

I even started working with Jenny at the shop. While I had money on the way, my miniscule savings had dwindled now that I wasn't living with the vampires. There was a part of me that missed the lap of luxury that was the mansion with its friendly butler and handsome men, but I liked the ritual of work, the mindless monotony of scanning objects and greeting customers. I had always been good at it, and it felt good to be something that I was good at.

I don't know why I was surprised when Zane came to see me at work, but I was.

I had been doing the late-night stocking, when the smattering of customers that came in were exhausted truck drivers or construction guys who either had to work too late or too early and were desperate for the coffee that we kept perpetually prepared. My hands were wrapped around a couple of aspirin bottles when I felt his approach.

"Hey, Zane," I said, not bothering to turn around. "What's up?"

"How did you know it was me?" he asked in that voice like liquid gold.

I shrugged, continuing to stock pain medications. "Because you feel different. All of you guys do."

I could almost feel him smile. I turned around and blinked. "What are you so dressed up for?"

Normally, Zane stuck to t-shirts and jeans. Of all the Sons of Vlad, Zane tended to look the most normal. His long, lanky body wasn't wearing a t-shirt and jeans now. Okay, the pants were jeans, but they were so dark and crisp I had to assume that they were new.

His button-down green shirt was done in plaid. He wore one of the bolo ties around his neck, like cowboys used to wear. Tucked under his arm was a picnic basket.

"Where's the horse?"

He smiled slowly. "It's been a long time since I had horses."

I blinked. "You were a cowboy?"

I thought Zane had been the oldest of them? I vaguely remembered someone telling me that. Cowboys were new in the grand scheme of the world. There was no way he could be a cowboy and the oldest of Vlad's offspring.

"No, but I roamed with them for a time."

"How?" I asked.

"Have dinner with me, and I'll tell you."

I hadn't gone on a date with any of the vampires since I'd moved out. I had this paranoid idea that they, as a group, had decided to give me the space that I had demanded. It was smart of them. I really didn't feel like dating.

But it seemed Zane was ready.

"What did you bring?"

I plopped the last medication bottle into place and ran my hands over the short work apron.

"Soup and sandwiches."

I raised my brow. I could never say no to a good sandwich. Add in soup, and I was done for. I took a tentative sniff. "Tomato?" I asked.

His grin was amused and cheerful. "And grilled ham and swiss."

I nearly melted into my shoes. After moving out, I had pretty much been living off a diet of prepackaged and take out. It wasn't that I couldn't cook; I wasn't half bad in that department. It was just easier to pick something up from the shop on my way out the door, and I'd been craving easy things recently.

"Sold. Come on, we can eat in the back."

He followed me, and after a little arranging, we turned the employee table into an impromptu dating spot.

"I have to admit I thought you'd put up more of a fight," he said as he poured the soup from a container into simple white bowls. "You made a point of leaving when you did."

I shrugged, swirling my spoon through the soup. "You brought food; that's fighting dirty."

He split a long baguette sandwich into two pieces and handed me half. I knew that vampires didn't have to eat. They could, and most of the guys did, but blood was the only way they stayed alive. I wondered how they were feeding, and who they were feeding on. I had been told that biting gave them power over a person. In fact, I had nearly been bitten during my first encounter with the vampires.

"I wanted my chance."

I put my spoon back into the soup without taking the taste that I had been looking forward to. "Why?"

He looked up at me; his grin was still on his lips, but it wasn't as bright. "Why?"

"Yes, why?"

He took a bite of his sandwich and chewed thoughtfully. "I could tell you it is because I want a woman."

I raised my brow at him. "Would you be telling the truth?

He shook his head. "No, I wouldn't. I like women; don't get me wrong, women are very nice. I prefer them. But getting women has never been all that hard for me."

I looked him over. I bet it didn't. Zane was, in a word, hot. Alan might be the most beautiful, but Zane had the kind of smoldering good looks that you expected a movie star to have. His long, lean body was made of nothing but muscle, and his smile could gleam. He also had just enough mystery swimming behind his eyes that most girls would just fall over themselves for a chance.

"So what is it?"

He pushed my food towards me. "Eat, please."

I gave him a look but brought my spoon to my lips. It was good. I took another bite, and he began to talk.

"I could say that it's the idea of having a capable woman like yourself as a companion. I could say a lot of things, but they would be lies. I try very hard not to lie. You saved my life, Lorena. I was nearly dead in that compound."

He had been. In an effort to break the prophecy, or rather transfer the prophecy from myself to my half-sister, they had taken the "born of vampire blood" part of it literally and tried to drain Zane completely. They had nearly succeeded, but, being a budding necromancer, I had felt him call out to me. I had saved him.

"So, this is...what? Repayment?"

He shrugged, his body moving like a panther inside of his plaid shirt. "Perhaps, but I don't like that word. You saved me; you rescued me from certain death, but in doing it, you saved us all."

I froze. "Wait, what?"

"Think about it. If the Order had succeeded in their creation, do you think magic would flow freely?"

I shook my head. "Well, no, that's sort of the point." Then, it hit me. "Oh, crap."

"Exactly. Without magic, we all die."

I shook my head. "All of you?"

"Our father has not been able to make a vampire in a century. I hear that the shifters are having trouble giving birth. Witches are being born weaker. I think, Lorena, that you and Jenny are the last witches that we have heard of being born. Magic is dying, slowly and surely it is. But you can save that; you can save us all, and if that means a child, then I will help you."

It was so bluntly stated. There was no romance offered, no promises of love. Just the steadfast certainty that he would help me save magic itself.

"What about love?"

He smiled and reached out, taking my hand in his. "You are a strong woman." When I opened my mouth to argue, he gripped my fingers a little tighter. "You rescued me at risk to yourself. That's brave. You haven't turned and run away after everything that's happened. That's strength. I like these qualities in a woman. You have imagination, you have kindness, and you care about others. Lorena, I do not love you right now, but I'd be a fool to think that, with a little time, I wouldn't fall for you."

My heart did a surprising dance inside of my chest. His words were good, very good. "You know me, but I don't know you."

"All you need to do is ask."

I opened and closed my mouth several times. All the questions I might have asked seemed to fall apart on my lips. "I...uhh…"

"I could start at the beginning, when I was human. I could tell you about my first fumbling years as a vampire. My favorite color, my favorite song."

I shook my head. Those were interesting thoughts, but at the end of the day, they were just statistics. After he had given me a rundown on the personality that he saw me having, I was more curious about his. Besides, after hearing Wei's sob story history, I wasn't sure that I wanted to know more about Zane's.

"Can all vampires do that voice thing?" I asked.

He ran his tongue across his lips and chuckled. "No. But I could do that when I was alive. I wasn't as good, but I have always had...a power of the voice."

I frowned. I wondered if all of the boys had their particular talents before they had been turned into vampires, and if those talents had just become heightened by becoming the undead. Or perhaps Vlad had picked them specifically for those talents.

"Really?"

"I was a speaker for my people."

"Who were your people?"

"They do not exist anymore. Most of them..." he went quiet for a moment. "Most of them were taken."

I didn't want to ask; it felt rude, but I found myself doing it anyway. "They were..." I fumbled.

He gave me a look. "Enslaved. Yes. They had been at war with another people, and, when many of our fighters were killed, they were sold to be taken to the New World. I was not. I was nearly dead, and thought that my life was over. Vlad saved me, and I wanted to save my people. I didn't, not then, but I tried."

I gripped his hand, still tucked in mine. I wanted to say that I was sorry. Slavery had been a craptacular thing, but "sorry" didn't cover it. "Sorry" was for spilling a cold drink in someone's lap, not for the buying and purchasing of people to the point that he didn't even have a group to call his own anymore.

"But that was how I got to be a cowboy," he said after a moment of tense quiet. "When I helped liberate what little was left of my family, they went west."

"Really?"

He nodded. "I know movies like to show that whole Clint Eastwood version of the west, but that's not true."

I was intrigued. "Tell me."

"About the west?"

I took another bite of my sandwich. "Why not?"

He shrugged. "You gotta remember that the West wasn't settled by the European colonists first. It had been settled by Native Americans, and later by Mexico, and finally by the Chinese who built the railroads, and the freedmen who worked alongside them. It wasn't an easy place to live, but the people who lived there were strong. I saw my people settled down in what would become New Mexico and helped build them a homestead. It was the least that I could do."

"That was good of you."

He shrugged. "Maybe. I felt bad because I couldn't stay. And I could only help at night."

"What did they think about you being a vampire?"

He shook his head. "They didn't care. I think they wouldn't have cared if I were a demon itself, so long as I helped them get away from a life that wasn't theirs."

"Where are they now?" I asked.

He gave me a look. "What do you mean?"

I shrugged. "Well, it's my opinion that a guy who went above and beyond to help his family out wouldn't just abandon them completely. I get this idea that you know exactly where their descendants are. In fact, I'm starting to think that family means a lot to you."

He grinned. "Well, you'd be right. I'd like to say I know where everyone is, and what they are doing, but the small group that settled in that farmstead have spread out everywhere. A few still live in the same farmhouse in New Mexico, but I don't know where they all are."

"Tell me about the ones you do know about."

He did. For the next few hours, I was treated to stories of a family I had never seen but soon began to know. Zane had a way of telling a story that helped me see Grandmother Celeste, who liked small yapping dogs, and her son Antoine, who tended to drink too much on Saturdays, but worked hard the rest of the week, and his wife Jasmine, who was very involved with the local church in spite, or perhaps because of, her husband's drinking. They had three children, all of whom still lived at home and helped out on the farm. They hosted a family reunion around the fourth of every year.

"You mean he ate all the pudding?" I asked, poking at the last few crumbs of my dinner.

He leaned forward, his broad hands on his knees. "The entire can! Grandma Celeste told him that if he was going to open that big can of pudding, he was going to eat the entire thing. He got stubborn about it; Antoine can be stubborn, and he got out a spoon and ate the whole five pounds."

I giggled. I couldn't help myself. I could picture this man I had never met with his face all screwed up with stubbornness shoveling one bite of pudding after another into his mouth while his mother looked on in staunch disapproval.

"He has not touched pudding since."

"I bet not," I said, standing up and stretching. My spine crackled in response. How long had I been sitting here? I glanced down at my watch. "Holy crap, it's nearly dawn. Jenny will be coming in on shift any moment. I need to get the coffee ready."

He stood up and started packing. "I'm sorry to keep you so late."

"It's fine," I promised, "I had a good time."

He looked at me then. "Did you?"

I thought about it. "Yes, I did. Dates with Alan were always big, and Dmitri was intense. I've never been on a date with Wei, but this...this was good."

"I'm glad."

He took my hand in his and brought it to his lips, pressing a tender touch there. "Can I see you tomorrow night?"

I thought about that too. Wei's words about being with Zane were echoing in my ears. Then again, what choice did I really have? Alan was so woefully in love with Dmitri that I just couldn't see myself being with him, no matter how pretty he was. And Dmitri needed some major anger management counseling before I even dabbed a toe in that pool. Then there was Wei, the guy I wanted but who didn't want me. Okay, that wasn't fair. He wanted me, but he didn't want to want me, and as far as I was concerned, that was pretty much the same thing.

So, my choices, as far as I knew, were Zane or no one.

"Yeah," I said, "alright. I am off tomorrow. Maybe we could go out."

"Just maybe?"

I rolled my eyes in amusement. "Okay, we can go out tomorrow. What did you want to do?"

"We'll figure that out when I pick you up. Dusk?"

"It's a date."

He vanished into the dawn like a shadow, and I watched him go.

~~

I'd like to say I spent the whole day thinking about my date with Zane, agonizing over where we would go and what I ought to wear. I didn't. I would also like to say that I had spent it sleeping. I hadn't slept a full night's sleep in a month. At best, I got a few hours in before I'd wake up all over again. On the plus side, I was on level 926 in Candy Crush, and my to-be-read pile was dwindling. My dreams were still weird. Instead, I spent it vegging out on the couch and reading more of my grandmother's journals. I had resisted the urge to skip forward to my birthday. It seemed unfair to her memory to miss all the things that she had thought about up until that moment.

So far, I had read about her graduating school and taking a job as a seamstress alongside my great-grandmother. About Jake, who I knew was the name of my grandfather, finally asking her out on a date and the slow romance that built between them.

May 12th 1975

Jake and I went out with his cousins and their girlfriends to Main Street Cafe. We got milkshakes, and we danced to a band playing there. It was fun. It's always fun with Jake, but he kept his distance, didn't even try to kiss me goodnight. The boy confuses me. I know, I absolutely know that he and I exchange vows, but I can't, for the life of me, see how we are supposed to get to the altar if he won't even make a grab for my hand.

May 27th 1975

I swear I don't care what my dreams have told me; I am through with that boy! I finally decided that I was a forward-thinking girl and flat out told Jake I wanted him to kiss me, and he went and got bug-eyed. Bug-eyed! Can you believe it?

And was it because he was a good Christian boy who wanted to wait until our wedding day to kiss me? Oh no, not even the slightest. He had been told that kissing a witch could kill a man. I could not believe my own ears! I asked him where he heard such poppycock and why on earth he had decided to go around with me if he never had any intention of ever kissing me.

Did I get an answer? Oh no, all he did was stumble over his words. It was as if he couldn't decide if he wanted to get mad at me or apologize. When I told him he could shove the piss poor apology that he was offering me where the sun didn't shine, he got all kinds of uppity.

He told me that I had put a spell on him! Can you believe it? He thought that he didn't really love me at all, but that I had used my witchy-ways to ensnare him. I told him that if I wanted to use magic to get a man, I would pick a far less idiotic one than him.

I have never been so rude as to walk away from someone when they were speaking to me, but I had no interest in listening to that foolish boy run his mouth any more. Maybe I'll go out with Richard Green. Now there is a boy who knows how to treat a woman, witch or otherwise.

I couldn't help but smirk to myself as I put the journal back down and wandered to the bathroom. My grandmother was feisty; I liked knowing that. I liked knowing that she didn't let people tread on her, and that she wasn't going to put up with stupid accusations. I also kind of liked that everything hadn't been so cut and dry for her.

A pang in my chest made me realize that I missed her. I missed this woman that I had never known. I wished she were here to talk to.

I plugged my curling iron in and lined up a bunch of my make-up on the top of my dresser, the one that used to be full of my grandmother's things.

"What are you doing?" Reikah asked. I hadn't heard her come in.

She was wearing one of my old pairs of jeans. They didn't fit her very well, but she couldn't wander around in her gray robes all of the time. She had taken some of my grandmother's clothes too. The top she wore would have looked more at home on a hippie, but she didn't seem to care what her clothes looked like.

"Getting ready. I'm going out with Zane tonight."

"Oh," she said, "will you sleep with him?"

I made a god-awful sound, like a monkey who had its tail stepped on. "What?"

"I assumed that is what this relationship is all about. To create a child. It would make more sense to get it over with, wouldn't it?"

I frowned at her. "Not for me. I'm kinda hoping the making of the baby is a fun part. Not just some...duty."

She shrugged. "Okay. I'm going out, anyway."

I looked at her. "You are?"

She nodded. "Jenny invited me to the Christmas concert at the school. Her cousins are participating."

"Oh."

She frowned at me. "What does that mean?"

How on earth was I supposed to tell her that Jenny had probably asked her out on a date? Did people with no interest in a physical relationship, as Reikah claimed, still go out on dates? Did the gender matter? Dear god, I needed to do some research before I shoved my foot in my mouth and said something incredibly rude.

"Is this a date?"

She shrugged. "I think she is interested, but I don't know if I am."

"Then why go on a date?"

"Are you interested in Zane?"

I had to think about that. I liked him, but I didn't know him well enough to say whether or not I was interested. "I could be."

"That's how I feel about Jenny."

I was confused, but it really wasn't my place to intervene. If they could end up in a happy relationship, then who was I to step in and make a mess of it? I looked her over. "Is that what you are wearing?"

She looked down at her clothing. "Is this the wrong outfit?"

I did my best not to wince, but I was pretty sure it showed on my face. "Well, if you two are just hanging out at home, I'd say it's fine, but you are going out for a Christmas pageant. It's kind of a big deal."

"I don't even know what a Christmas Pageant is."

"It's like a show with food. Everyone goes to a big community location; you'll be going to the school, and you watch the kids put on some kind of holiday-themed play, and then everyone sits down to a great big meal together. They've been doing them forever. My grandmother wrote about them in her journals."

She tugged at her shirt. "So..."

"I'll help you."

We spent the next thirty minutes helping one another get ready. Or rather, I helped her, and she did her best to help me. She was tiny. I tended towards the size ten side of things. Reikah, at best, was a size six. I didn't have a whole lot that worked. She was also self-conscious about showing off her legs. I guess all those years wearing gray robes had some lingering effects.

We found a green dress, a little outdated but long enough to satisfy her and festive enough to satisfy me. Then I began the long process of explaining make-up and the application thereof.

I'm no wizard with such things, but I knew enough to know that Reikah would never need more than a little to look amazing. Her skin was fantastic, and her eyes were already dark-lashed. All we did was add a little shadow to the lids and gloss to the lips.

For myself, who had no clue where I was going, I wore my nicest pair of jeans and a turtleneck in the same not-quite-blue and not-quite-green color as my eyes. I went a little heavier on the make-up, but I needed to cover up the circles beneath my eyes from lack of sleep.

God, I really wanted to sleep.

With a quick sweep of my brush through my hair, I decided that I was ready enough when the door knocked. It was too early for it to be Zane.

"Will you answer it?" Reikah asked, pulling out a few pins for her hair.

"Sure."

I wandered to the living room, a ghost cat in my wake, and opened the door for Jenny. She looked nervous, beautiful as always, but nervous. She peeked over my shoulder as I crossed my arms and leaned against the door frame.

"So," I said, raising my brow, "when were you going to tell me you were going on a date?"

She looked sheepish. "It's not a date, not really."

"Funny, because I just spent forty minutes helping her get ready. I don't do that when friends, or bicker buddies really, are just going to hang out."

"I thought she might want to see the Christmas Pageant."

I nodded. "I heard. So, this is just fun, then? Should I go tell her to change out of the vintage dress?"

"Don't you dare." Jenny charged up one step until the two of us were eye-to-eye. "Shoot, am I making some kind of mistake?"

I shook my head. "No, but talk with her before things go too far. Lots of talking."

She grinned. "What's a relationship without some kind of communication?"

I was going to have to accept that. Reikah chose that moment to come out of the room. I knew Reikah had come out because Jenny's eyes went wide and she seemed to completely forget that I existed. I was a little offended; then, I turned and realized that I couldn't blame the girl. Reikah looked amazing.

"H-hi there," Jenny, who always knew what to say and brimmed with confidence, stuttered.

"Are you ready?" Reikah asked.

"Oh, yes."

I got a series of goodbyes before they piled into Jenny's car and headed off into the evening. I wished them all the best. Maybe if they worked out, the rest of us stood some kind of chance.

The sun dipped below the horizon, and a shape began to form in front of me.

"Wow, that was prompt -- oh." I cut off abruptly when I realized the vampire forming in front of me was not Zane; it was Wei.

He was wearing what I referred to as his workout clothes, better thought of as a martial arts uniform, but not the terry cloth ones they had in modern shops, but older and more...I don't know...real. I looked him over; in each hand, he held a short staff.

"Lorena?" he asked.

"Yeah, what are you doing here?"

"I thought...we would continue your lessons."

I blinked. Right up until our random make-out sessions, Wei had been teaching me martial arts. I had never thought of myself as the kind of person who wanted to learn Kung Fu, but Wei was an excellent teacher, and it made me feel kinda powerful to learn how to move my body in a fight. Not that I had any expectations of getting into a hand-to-hand battle, but you never really knew.

"Tonight?" I asked.

His eyes traveled over my outfit. It wasn't a flashy getup, but it wasn't my normal jeans and a gamer shirt either.

"You have plans."

"She does."

Oh, this was good, I thought to myself as Zane appeared a few feet behind Wei. I nearly laughed. We were dressed similarly. Both of us wore slacks and a turtleneck, but he had added a vest to his. Wei's face went completely blank.

"I see."

I should have bit my tongue. I even told myself I didn't need to say anything. But my mouth had its own ideas. "What the hell is that supposed to mean?"

"It means nothing. I am glad to see that you are taking my advice." His lip curled ever so slightly before returning to that perfect empty mask.

"Advice?" I spat the word back at him. I wasn't sure why I was so angry. No, I wasn't angry. I was pissed. I knew he was mad. Oh, he could hide it with his face all he wanted, but I was a necromancer, and I could feel his thoughts swimming against my skin. He wasn't okay. He was upset. What right did he have to be upset? "Is that what you call flat out telling me that I should take Zane as my prophecy partner?"

Zane stayed quiet, folding his hands neatly behind his back as he watched us. He might have been a tall dark statue. Wei's fingers tightened hard enough on the staff to make the wood creak.

"What would you call it?" he demanded.

I fumbled. I knew words. I was okay with them. I read a lot, but I couldn't think of a single term for what he had done, I just knew that I was mad about it. "I'd call it the weirdest ultimatum ever. Have this guy or nothing; that's pretty much what you did."

"It is your best choice."

"It's not my choice if you are the one making it."

His eyes flamed, but his face remained utterly impassive. I was so mad about that. Tears, for reasons I couldn't explain, were popping into my eyes, and the only thing keeping them back was the knowledge that I would ruin my half an hour's worth of make-up.

He bowed. "It was wrong of me to arrive without announcement." His shape began to lose form.

I shot my hand out and grasped at that magic that made him the undead. My own particular power surged through me and coiled around him, locking him in place. "Oh, no you don't. You aren't pulling that disappearing crap on me again. You've done that to me twice already, dammit. You are going to stay here, and you are going to listen to me.

You love me. I know it. I don't understand it, but I know it. I can feel it every time you look at me, but you won't let yourself have it because you are so afraid of losing it. Well, I got news for you buster; fear is a part of love. You are always afraid that you might not be good enough, that you might screw it up, that you might lose them, but for the love of crap, that's just the way it is. You want me...say so."

He gave me a look that was half heartache and half anger. Those tears I'd been holding back ran down my cheeks and ruined the perfect wings of my liner. Damn.

"You don't love me."

I wasn't entirely sure about that. "You haven't given me the chance."

I dropped him as suddenly as my magic had scooped him up. "You are so afraid you won't even give me that. You know what? No. I'm done with this. I'm done with you. You kiss me, you touch me, you light my whole body on fire and then you leave me because I make you afraid. I could forgive you the first time, maybe even the second time, but this? Now...no. Yes. I choose Zane. I choose him, and you can go home and tell the others."

Wei opened his mouth and then snapped it shut. He bowed once to me, and began to vanish. I was almost sure I saw a tear run down his face as he left.

I crumpled to the ground and started to cry.

CHAPTER EIGHT

Zane and I wound up sitting on the couch while I just let it all out. I know it's pretty declassee or whatever to talk to guy B about guy A, but I couldn't help it right that moment. I was so upset. How dare he. How dare he just show up here unannounced and get that cold face thing going. I wasn't down for that.

Crap, I wished he had stayed. I wished, just a little, he had fought to stay.

Zane, surprisingly, wasn't upset.

"Go ahead," he said, "cry it all out."

He wrapped his arms around me and pulled me close. I laid my head on the firm line of his chest and stretched my legs out. "This is not how I thought tonight was going to go."

"It's okay. There are other nights. Just let it all out."

So I did. I told him everything. Heck, I went all the way back to the very first moment that I had walked through the front door of my grandmother's house all the way up until this most recent sob session. I don't know why I did. All I really needed to tell him was that Wei was a jerk and I wasn't sleeping well. I think the only thing I left out was the unknown sender texts. They weren't all that important anyway.

"When was the last time you got a good night's sleep?"

I laughed, and laughing through my tears caused me to hiccup. "I don't even know."

"Alright, new plan; we are staying in tonight."

He patted my hip and got up, going to my fridge to see what was there. The next thing I knew, he was pushing a glass of orange juice into my hands. I love orange juice. It's the elixir of life. I took a sip and felt a little better.

"You need a plan," he said evenly.

I nodded. "That's true."

"But you need a good meal and a good night's sleep first."

"You think?"

"I know."

He pushed some things around my fridge. "When was the last time you went grocery shopping?"

"What's a couple weeks short of never?" I asked, taking another sip.

"Okay, finish your juice. Then, we are going shopping."

I raised my brow at him. "We got dressed up all cute so that we could go shopping?"

"You think I'm cute?"

I rolled my eyes. "You know you are cute."

"Do I?"

I sighed and took another long sip of my drink. "You aren't like Alan, who wears his attractiveness on his velvet sleeves for all to see, but no man wears a turtleneck and a silk vest on a first date unless he is very sure of everything beneath those clothes."

He laughed and shook his head. "It's a second date, but you aren't wrong. I know what I look like, what women think of me. But more than that, I want you to have a full fridge."

"Why?"

He hesitated. "Perhaps you forgot, but you just stated that you had picked me. Your health, all of it, means something to me."

I had, hadn't I? I waited to feel something about that. I should, right? I should feel nervous or relieved, or maybe a mesh of the two. I didn't. The only feeling that I felt was exhaustion.

"Oh."

He raised his brow, crossing his arms over his chest. "Oh? That's what you have to say? Oh?"

I ran a hand over my face. "I'm a terrible human being, but yes. That's all I've got right this moment. I don't think it's all sunk in yet."

"Did you mean it?" he asked.

My mouth clapped closed, and I thought about it. Had I meant it? Well, I had certainly meant it in the heat of the moment, when all I could think was that I was done with whatever was happening between Wei and myself. That I was done with the other guys and all of their melodrama. My only option was Zane, and he wasn't a bad option.

He was attractive, of course; all of the Sons of Vlad were. He seemed kind-hearted enough. And I liked the honesty that he had shown me so far.

"Yes," I said after a moment, "I did."

He set aside the few measly remnants of food that he had found in the fridge and reached over to me, taking my hands in his. He brought them up to his lips, kissing one set of knuckles and then the other.

"You will not regret this choice."

I hoped not. I was still of the mindset that making a child, no matter how the parents felt about each other, created a bond. In some people, that bond wasn't all that great, but in some, it could be the beginning of something good.

Oh god, I thought to myself, *did he mean that I wouldn't regret it right away?* Maybe he did. Oh boy. I was so not ready for that right this moment.

His grin was sudden and bright. "I'm not going to throw you over my shoulder and take you to the bedroom, Lorena." He gave my hands a gentle squeeze. "We can take this as slow as you need to."

I blushed hard enough to make my head feel a little light. "I wasn't thinking that. Okay," I amended, "I wasn't thinking that exactly. Actually, I was thinking about how you used your vampire mojo on me."

He dropped one hand and took my chin gently between two cool fingers, lifting until my gaze met his. His eyes were so golden. I'd always thought of them as hawk's eyes, but now that I was looking, they were more like pieces of polished amber, with all the brightness of those precious stones. There was such depth there, such warmth and strength too.

"I will never make you do something you do not wish to do. I will only use that power on you to keep you from harm, as long as you, little necromancer, promise the same."

No, I said to myself, he was not a bad option at all.

I nodded, cleared my throat, and took a step back. The moment had too much heft to it, and what I didn't need more of right this moment was another reason to feel like the weight of the world was existing solely on my shoulders.

"Okay, I can promise you that." I answered, shoving my hands in the barely existent pockets of my slacks. "So, you said something about the grocery store?"

He nodded. "You need to take care of yourself, Lorena. You need to eat well, sleep well, and relax. Yes," he said, holding up a single hand when I opened my mouth to argue, "I know that your work and your studies matter to you, but that does not mean that you can ignore the basics of caring for yourself. I will step in if your actions cause you harm."

There was something about the way he phrased those words that left a sour taste in my mouth, but I was too tired to really analyze why.

"Okay."

We, and by "we" I mean I, pulled on some cold weather jackets. There wasn't any snow on the ground yet, but the sky was the particular shade of gray that promised it. The ground was frozen beneath my boots. If it did snow, it would stick.

We climbed into my car and drove the half a dozen miles to the grocery store in silence. Sometimes, silence was a bad thing, a heavy, sour silence that said that people were mad or uncomfortable. Then there was the lighter silence of comfort. This silence was somewhere in between. I wanted to talk to him, ask him questions, but I didn't know what to ask.

So, being me, I decided to go for broke and ask the most awkward thing I could ask. "How did my sister get you to the compound since she isn't a necromancer?"

He didn't blush. I don't think that vampires could blush. But there was a tightening to his cheeks that told me that he was embarrassed by the question.

"I don't mean to pry, but it's been hanging on my mind for a while."

He swallowed. "I...we..."

I hadn't known Zane for very long, but hearing him stumble over his words had me glancing over at him.

"Zane?"

"She offered me a taste of her blood."

I blinked. "Really?"

He ran his hands across his knees. "Every vampire has a weakness to a certain kind of blood. Something that tastes a little better to us. I do not know what it is for the others, but for me...for me, mages have the sweetest flavor."

"Oh," I said, swallowing. "She used her neck as bait."

He was quiet enough that I knew there was more to the story that he wasn't telling me.

"Spill it," I said, navigating into a space in the parking lot. "What happened?"

"Lorena, I-"

I shook my head. "Listen, I just promised that you and I are going to end up making a life together; I think that's a fairly big deal. The least that you can offer in return is honesty."

He sighed. "I had tasted from her several times. We had been..."

A thought hit me. A really terrible thought. One of those thoughts that, once it happened, did not just disappear. "Oh...Oh, Zane. Say it isn't so."

"We had been intimate. I thought, perhaps, that we were lovers."

"You slept with my sister?"

It bothered me. I knew it shouldn't. He hadn't known me when he'd been nibbling on her. There was no logic in me mentally flinching away because of it. Yet there I was, trying really hard not to imagine Zane sinking his fangs into Connie's freckled shoulder.

"You asked for honesty."

I turned the key in the ignition, and for a minute, we sat in my car in complete silence.

"Did you...care about her?" I asked.

He hesitated for a moment. "I did."

Ugh. Why did I have to ask for honesty? Honesty sucked. It was full of hard truths and harder facts. I didn't like it. Give me a pretty lie any day. Wonder Woman would be really disappointed with me.

I leaned forward and pressed my forehead to the top of the steering wheel. "Ugh."

"Should I apologize?"

"Do you feel bad about it?"

He shook his head. "I feel bad that the knowledge hurts you."

Fair enough. I sighed and shook my head. "Well, not going to lie, it bugs me. But you've got two things working in your favor."

He eyed me. "Oh?"

"The first is that we got this out before anything really happened between us. If you'd told me after, I'd be a lot more upset."

"And the second," he asked when I went quiet.

I slapped my fingers over the seat belt. "The second thing going for you is that killer Superman smile you've got going on."

The grin he flashed me was worthy of the Man of Steel himself.

"That's the one." I opened my door and slid out of the car. "Come on, let's go make me a responsible adult."

Being with Zane wasn't hard, even with the knowledge of him drinking on my half-sister's neck. We wandered through all the aisles of the grocery supercenter and stocked up as if the apocalypse was coming. We didn't talk about anymore hard topics for the most part. But somewhere around the frozen food section, I had to ask.

"Do you still care about her?"

He hooked his thumbs in the loops of his slacks. The shining buckle at his belt shimmered. "It's hard to care about someone who tried to bleed you dry."

"That's not a 'no.'"

He blew out a deep breath. "Honesty?"

I hesitated. "Yeah, honesty."

"When a being, any being, who lives a long time grows to care for a person, it is very hard for them to stop."

Damn. He still liked my sister. Gross. I couldn't have any fuzzy feelings for a guy, vampire or otherwise, who was into my sister. So, what if they weren't dating anymore? At least, I assumed they weren't dating. There were a lot of ways to say that a relationship was over; attempting to completely exsanguinate someone was definitely on that list.

"Okay. I appreciate your honesty."

"But you don't like what I said," he asked as I piled a bunch of frozen pizzas into the cart. He eyed them but smartly didn't say anything.

"No, I don't. But...well...it's better than you saying it's over when it isn't. How long?"

He gave me a look. "How long what?"

"How long were you and her a thing?"

He thought it over. I wondered how long was too long or not long enough. "A year."

I knitted my brows. "Wait, she's only known for like...three months. Not even."

He nodded, and it was then that I saw the raw pain in his eyes. "I know."

Shoot. There was love there, real love, and real pain. It was going to take him a long time to get over that. Did it take vampires longer to get over their feelings? I would have to assume so. Wei flashed into my mind, and his confusion of feelings. Double shoot.

When we drove back home, the silence was heavy and sour.

CHAPTER NINE

In this dream, I was lying on a table that was familiar and nightmarish. It was the table that I had found Zane on all those weeks ago at the compound. Tubes were hooked into my skin, and the floor beneath me was covered in blood. I didn't like this table. I didn't like this place. I tried to tug myself free, but nothing would move.

Connie's face peered down at me. That perfect Irish cream color bedecked with freckles. Were we really sisters? Here I was with dark hair and sallow skin, thanks to the tubes, and hazel eyes; she was looking like the pin-up child for the freckled red-head.

"What do you want?" I asked, feeling sick to my stomach.

"I want your destiny."

No. She couldn't have that. She could have pretty much anything but that. I knew what she'd do with my destiny; she'd screw it all up. Magic would be saved for the hands of the chosen few. And, as far as I was concerned, that pretty much sucked.

"You can't have it."

She sneered down at me. "You will use my castoff to create a world I loathe?"

Who the heck talked like that? And seriously, when did Connie talk at all? I had always known her to be quiet. Then again, maybe I had never known her. I hadn't thought that she'd had much in the way of romantic relationships; even Jenny had said she'd never seen Connie with anyone. Apparently, my half-sister had been carrying on an illicit relationship under everyone's nose. Had my mother been involved? Had she pushed it to happen?

"Wow," I said with a hint of snappiness, "sounding kind of bitter there, little sister. You mad that your ex is taking me out?"

She gave me a look that told me she was pissed, but nothing else. "I never cared about him."

I shrugged and laid back against the seriously uncomfortable bed. "Sure. Whatever you say."

"I am not you. I don't drool over the dead."

A thought snapped into my unconscious mind. "That's weird, because apparently you were drooling over him before I was part of the picture."

Her eyes went bright. It wasn't the kind of brightness that a vampire could get, but there was magic there, wild and angry and brimming behind her eyes. "I will kill you. I will take your destiny."

I yawned. I added in what little stretch the tubes attached to me, slowly draining my life, could offer. "Yeah. Sure. Whatever. You keep breaking into my dreams and making these crappy promises, and I will just lay here and wait for that to happen. Sound good?"

She howled, and it was the sound of a wolf. The large, sharp-toothed dog that followed her about joined her. The sound of their mingled voices was, in a word, creepy.

"Don't make light of what I could do to you."

I sighed. "I'm not making light of it. I promise. I'm just a little over this constant melodrama. "You don't like what the prophecy says I'll do with magic, and I don't like how you keep trying to kill me. It's all very hum-drum."

"Being flippant won't get you anywhere."

"Neither will be putting your word-a-day dictionary to use, but here we are."

She began to change. I had seen Dmitri shift when he was losing control; this was both the same and different. With Dmitri, the transition was terrifying but smooth, as if watching someone stretch clay. With Connie, everything snapped and broke. I heard the popping of bones and tendons crackling. Her teeth, as normal and human as mine, fell out of her head as sharper ones burst through her gums, leaving them bloody.

Her skin, pale as a spring morning, began to turn dark. Not human dark, not a pleasant shade of brown, but the dark of shadows between burnt trees. It ate up the creamy flesh and the freckles with it, turning her into the color of coal smudges. Fur burst forth, as dark and shadowy as the rest of her, and her eyes went from their normal human shade to brilliant red.

Fear danced down my spine, and I squirmed against the table. I was suddenly aware of the cold needles stuck into my flesh. The lightness, the flippancy went away.

"You take what's mine?" she snarled, snapping her sharp teeth as she leaned over me. Her breath was terrible, like rotten meat. "I'll take what's yours."

She lowered those sharp teeth to my exposed belly, and opened her mouth wide. I waited to feel the pricking of them against my skin. It was going to hurt. I was sure of it.

The yowl of a cat tore me out of the nightmare.

Maahes was sitting on my chest, his familiar weight a great comfort as he stared down into my eyes. He bent and thumped his head against my face, making me aware of tears streaming down my cheeks.

"Hey," I said, my voice shaking. "How are you doing that?"

He licked at the tear trail. I could feel the roughness of his tongue, but the water remained behind. I wrapped my arms around him as I sat up, holding him against me.

"That was a weird one, buddy."

He struggled against my grip for a moment before curling in on himself and making a ball in my lap. He started to purr, and I gave him a few shaky-handed pets. I ached. It wasn't as bad as the last time, not by a long shot, but I still felt terrible, like I had the world's worst cold. A glance at my clock told me that I had only been asleep for four hours. I wouldn't even have gotten that if I hadn't been so exhausted that I'd broken down and taken one of the sleeping pills that I found in the cabinet. Who would have thought that a witch would have sleeping pills?

I took a deep breath and shook my head hard enough to clear the cobwebs. "Okay," I said, sliding out of the bed. "It's time to look through the grimoire."

My grandmother's book of shadows, or magical grimoire, was chock full of information about all kinds of magical things. I'd nearly forgotten it since I had Jenny and her grandmother teaching me witchcraft and Reikah teaching me wizardry. Then, I had been pouring over my grandmother's journals. But it was well past time for me to learn something about dreams.

The book was large and heavy, and I kept it in the second drawer of my grandmother's dresser. My clothes didn't even take up half the drawers, so it fit nicely enough. I dragged it out and plopped it on the bed along with myself. Maahes sat next to me, eyeing the pages with feline curiosity.

"What do you think, Maahes?" I asked, as I began flipping through the pages. There was no index, and the book must have had three or four hundred pages, making it hard to navigate. It was made out of hand-stitched leather, with a large five-pointed star on the front. Each point of the star, which sat inside of a circle, was marked with a particular triangle symbol. I knew now that each triangle was associated with one of the major elements; Earth, Air, Fire, and Water. It didn't help that the inside of the book was put together in a whimsical fashion, as if my grandmother had just written things down as she had learned them. "Anything on dreams in here?"

The cat eyed me and then the book. He bumped his nose against it and, by magic, the pages began to turn. They moved fast enough to have my hair fluttering out of my face.

When the pages stopped, it was about two thirds of the way through the book on a page labeled Somniamancy.

"Holy crap," I whispered, looking at Maahes, "how did you do that?"

He looked at me with all the intensity of the feline gaze, and then he sat back, shot one foot in the air, and began cleaning the inside of his thigh.

"Helpful," I said with a roll of my eyes.

While Maahes bathed himself, I turned my attention back to the book, reading aloud to myself. "Somniamancy, or the magic of dreams, is split into several schools of magic. The first is Dream Walking, or the ability to insert oneself into the dreams of others in order to manipulate them or discern something about the target.

This can be done by many witches, and used for good or ill. The next is Dream Prophecy, where your dreams are glimpses into the future or warnings for things to come. Dreams of Prophecy are often naturally occurring in a small percentage of witches. Those who have the gift of Prophecy can cause prophetic dreams by utilizing dream teas. The last, and most uncommon, is the ability to craft a Dreamscape.

"A Dreamscape is another dimension, accessible only by the unconscious mind. A Dreamscape is created by a Somniamancer, and is, in its own way, as real as the world we live in. The scape itself is malleable, as most dreams are, but the pain inflicted in these dreams is real, up to and including death. To die in a dreamscape is to be cut from one corporeal body and thus die here in the terra realm.

"Somniamancers are rare, and their gifts can be used for either good or ill. When used for good, the Somniamancer can help a person suffering from trauma or insomnia get a good night's sleep and work through their difficulties. It is said that a good night's sleep in the lap of a Dream Mage is the greatest sleep that a person can have.

"However, when used for ill, a Somniamancer's gift can be terrifying. They can trap a victim in a world of nightmares, using a person's fears against them. It is important to note that the longer one is in a dreamscape crafted at their hands, the harder it is to break free of what they have created. It also becomes easier and easier for a Somniamancer to touch one's dreams the more often the unconscious contact happens."

I paused, keeping my finger on the page. Somniamancer, a dream mage…it wasn't something I had ever heard of, not even in all of the video games that I had played. There were some fantasy books I could think of that had a wizard who could mess with dreams, but that was about it.

Was that what was happening to me? Was some dream mage messing with my head? I scanned ahead a few pages, most which had to do with dream prophecy, no surprise considering my grandmother's gift.

"When a Somniamancer with ill intent turns their attentions on a particular person, the victim may begin to experience bouts of insomnia followed by a deep sleep with strange dreams that leave them feeling more exhausted when they wake up."

Well, I thought to myself, that solved that problem. Someone with dream magic was screwing around with my head. But who? And why? I could make a couple of educated guesses about why. They were part of the Order, and they didn't want me to fulfill the prophecy. Or they weren't part of the Order, but they still didn't want me to fulfill the prophecy.

"Okay, how do I fight it?" I asked the book, using my finger to scroll over the pages, careful not to smudge the long-since-dry ink. "In the early stages, a Somniamancer can be fought via the use of sigils and herbal magic. Drawing protective sigils on your brow, wrists, and across the chest will offer a first line of defense, and stuffing sachets of protective herbs beneath your pillow and body before going to sleep will offer a second line."

"Well, guess what I'm going to learn to do today, Maahes?"

Finished with his bath, Maahes stretched out next to me, rolling over to offer his stomach for a rub. I gave it.

Then, his ears pricked forward and he rolled over.

"What?" I asked, following the line of his gaze.

It was still dark outside, being that it was winter and not even four thirty in the morning, but I could see the shape of a man standing across the street. I remembered, months ago, seeing another man standing out there, the first night that I had moved in.

But, once my imagination stopped running wild, I realized that I knew this shape.

I opened the window. "Wei? What are you doing here?"

He turned, looking at me.

He was so damn pretty, I thought. Why did he have to be so pretty? His rounded face, dark hair, and darker eyes just seemed to call to me, though I'd be lying to myself if I thought my attraction was purely physical. I liked his control and his discipline, two things that I didn't have even on the best of days. I liked that, even after all this time, he still cared about something that happened in his past. I liked how he made me feel safe, and I liked how he made me feel...good.

I sighed. "You know hanging outside sleeping girls' windows in the middle of the night is a vampire novel trope, right? I mean, that's pretty terrible, even for an angsty vampire like you."

He frowned at me. "I'm not angsty."

I snorted. "You are the angstiest guy I have ever met, and I was in high school while the scene kids were there."

He frowned. "I worried."

"Come inside; it's too cold out there for this conversation."

I stepped away from the window, and, as a mist of smoky brown, he spilled into my grandmother's bedroom.

"Handy," I said once he had formed again. "Can you hear when you are made of mist? Or do you need ears?"

"I can hear just fine."

"So why not stay mist? Unless you wanted me to see you haunting my road."

He shook his head. "It takes a great deal of concentration to stay incorporeal."

"Ah." I crossed my arms and sat on the corner of the bed. Maahes was nowhere to be seen. "So what are you doing being an undead stalker?"

"I wasn't stalking. I was...wandering..."

I raised my brow. "And you just happened to wander my way?"

He shrugged his shoulders. He wore green tonight. He looked amazing in green. Heck, he looked amazing in all the colors that he liked to wear: green, blue, black, or red. Heck, he'd probably look fine in a burlap sack. "It was not intentional." He turned away from me as if he didn't want to look at me anymore.

"Okay."

I sighed and stood up. I surprised us both by wrapping my arms around his middle and laying my head on his back. He went vampire still beneath my cheek, and I held him closer.

"I'm sorry for yelling at you."

He relaxed just a little. "I deserved it."

I smiled, but it was a sad smile. "I wish you were okay with being mine."

He breathed out. "I do too."

We stayed like that for a long while. Then, I stepped back. "Okay, time for a lesson."

"A what?"

"A martial arts lesson. You don't think I've given up, do you? There are creepy people after my butt. I gotta be ready for them."

He turned around and eyed me. I didn't understand the look that he gave me, but it felt like he was trying to figure out something. I knew I could figure it out. All I'd have to do is push a tendril of my magic out to him and I'd know everything that he was thinking, but the fact was I was too nervous to know what was going on behind those eyes. I didn't want to know.

"As you wish."

He moved towards the front door, and I paused. "You...wanna fight outside?"

He eyed me. "Is there a problem?"

"Maybe not for you, Mr. My Heart Doesn't Beat, but I'm a living breathing woman, and it's all of twenty degrees out there. I'll freeze my butt off."

He raised one brow at me, and the tiniest glint of humor flickered through his gaze. "Do you think your enemies will care if it is twenty below? Or colder?"

Ugh. I hated that he had a point. "Fine. But if I get hypothermia, you are going to feel really bad."

He nodded. "I will."

I ignored the tiny little jump in my chest that liked the fact that he'd feel bad. It was stupid to feel anything like that, anything even close to that now that I had told Zane that I was going to be with him. I made some comment about putting on real clothes rather than pajamas, and Wei gave me the space to change.

When I was ready, I followed Wei's back outside and towards the small patch of land that was behind my grandmother's place and to one side of the garage. There was a little square of wood, about ten by ten, that would have made for a nice garden if it weren't the middle of winter. As it was, my boots crunched over the frozen earth.

My breath came out in misty clouds as Wei and I began to move together. The beginning of our lessons always started with the Kata. Kata might have been a Japanese word, but it was practiced in forms of Chinese martial arts too. In slow, controlled movements, we took our bodies through a series of strikes, blocks, and turns. It was almost like a dance, but by the time it was over, I had forgotten that it was cold.

I was, however, intensely aware of him. I was aware of the way his lips were parted ever so slightly, the way his braided hair swung nearly the length of his back. I closed my eyes, trying not to think of him, but when I opened them, my eyes had slipped into magic sight.

A witch, and a few other magical beings, could see magic. Most people, if magic was cast around them or even against them, couldn't see anything. But a witch could see the lines that wove through the earth. The last time I had done this it had been mid-fall, and everything had been living. Now, with winter sliding along our part of the world, the lines were foggy and muted. I glanced down at myself and resisted the urge to gasp.

Usually, my magic looked like a snarled bit of thread, sliding through me in shades of gold and pale shimmering blue. I had been working on fixing that, but tonight...tonight, it was different, completely different. There were tinges of green throughout my own cords of magic, and while the source was no longer one big ball of cat-trounced yarn, it was savaged, broken in some places. The few tendrils I had that slithered from me all reached towards Wei.

As soon as it was over, he struck out at me. I moved out of the way.

"Do not let magic distract you," he said.

He struck at my middle, and the air whooshed from my lungs, but I had pulled away just enough that I wasn't completely breathless.

The lines of magic that made up Wei were the same icy blue that interwove itself with my gold, but his had tinges of obsidian and ruby mixed in with his. All the vampires had the red; I think it is the magic that made them what they were, but I wondered what the blue and black were about. As I focused on them, I realized something. I could see where he was going to move just a fraction of a moment before he did it.

He struck, and I blocked. He tried to feint, but I knew where the real hits were coming from. I couldn't seem to land a strike on him either, as much as I tried. His skill was pretty incredible, what with there being a few hundred years of practice and some super natural biology behind it. But with my intuition and his skill, the two of us were locked into a series of movements with neither one of us getting any ground on the other.

"You've been practicing," he said.

"Yes."

I hadn't been practicing martial arts, not without him, but I had been practicing magic, and that apparently was giving me an edge. I didn't know it could, but now that I did, I wondered just what else could happen. As I thought that, I sent a tendril of that particular necromantic magic to my fist and hit hard.

It connected with his face. He went flying backwards. He didn't stay down long at all, barely more than a second, but when he stood up, there was a tiny line of red beneath his nose. I hadn't known a vampire could bleed.

"It has been a long time since a person has drawn my blood." He looked a little surprised. To be fair, I was pretty surprised myself.

"Sorry?"

The look of shock in his eyes was replaced by stubbornness and pride. God, there was something so lovely about him when he got all stubborn about something. Maybe it was some wild streak in me, but I liked it.

I was so busy watching his eyes that I didn't see his leg sweep out and take my stance. I tumbled back, but I dragged him with me, sending us both to the cold ground.

His body landed on top of mine, and we both went still. I could feel his masculinity pushing against me and I ground against it, spreading my thighs to feel him that much better. He made a sound like a hungry animal, and I reveled in it. A single drop of his blood touched my skin, and my magic flared. It spilled through me white hot and vibrating. I was aware of everything: the cold ground at my back, the press of his body against mine, every flicker of color in his eyes. I could see every lash of magic through the world around me no matter how small or minute. I could feel them all flowing. I could have pulled them to me if I wanted.

Then, it all pulsed, and I was blind with the power. The world faded, and all I could see were Wei's vampire eyes staring at me, a light of magic spilling out of them like shadows dancing in his gaze. I squirmed again, not just from the feeling of him so close, but from the itchy sensation of trying to hold all of this power inside of myself. It sought something, someplace to go.

Wei's mouth slid along my neck, and I purred.

"Yes, Wei, yes," I gasped, offering my neck to him. I could feel the hard press of his teeth. His hands gripped my shoulders, and he held me down against the unforgiving ground. I could hear my pulse in my ears, fast and frantic, and I knew he could too.

"Lorena," he whispered against my skin.

"Do it," I purred. I had no idea that I wanted to be bitten so badly, but right this moment, there was very little that I, or the magic that spilled through me, wanted more.

He shivered once and pulled away. I hated that. I hated that he could pull away when all I wanted to do was give in. I grabbed him and pulled him back and begged him. What I said I don't remember, but whatever it was, it worked.

The bite was hard, almost violent, but it was bliss.

My magic poured into him, spilled life into him. He went warm against me first, the gold of his skin taking on a rosy hue as his body filled with my blood. I felt his heart pound beneath the hand that I pressed to his chest, a wild beat to match my own. I felt him suck on my neck, and it made parts of me I had too long ignored flare to life, hungry for some touch, some attention. When he pulled his head back from my neck, his teeth red and exposed, the lower half of him ground against me, and I shivered in response.

"Lorena," he whispered again, followed by something in a language I didn't know, but it had the elegant rhythm of Mandarin; then again, it could have been whatever his mother tongue was.

"Wei," I said back, "please."

My body had never felt so alive, and to that point, neither had his. I pushed myself against him, and his hips jerked automatically.

"No," he whispered, pulling back. "I cannot."

"Why the heck not?"

He laughed. I didn't expect it, but he looked down at me and saw the expression of complete and total exasperation, and he laughed. Then, as quickly as it'd started, it had cooled. "Because you do not belong to me. You do not love me."

I growled. "So?"

He pushed a hair out of my face, his lips so close to mine that I was sure he was going to kiss me. "We both know that matters a great deal. I cannot."

"Because of...her?" I said, unwilling to say the name of his long dead wife.

He slid away from me. "Yes, in part. But because you have promised yourself to Zane."

I blinked. Oh, right. I totally had done that. How could I have forgotten? God, what kind of person was I that I forgot a promise that I had made all of seven hours or so ago? A terrible kind of person, that's who. I cursed vehemently and surged to my feet.

"Crap, crap. What are we going to tell him?"

"The truth," he said matter-of-factly.

Right. There was that. There was a conversation I really didn't want to have. Hey, Zane, I know we just started this potential relationship, but I totally got to second base with Wei, or is fangs third base? I dunno, you're the vampire. You tell me. Nope. Definitely not.

"Ohhh, this is gonna suck." The word 'suck' brought a blush to Wei's cheeks that I would have found amusing were it not for the ache in my neck. Man, that was going to be one hell of a hickey. "Not funny."

He grinned. "It is a little funny."

"Where the heck is this sense of humor coming from?" I demanded. "My Wei is all stoic and grumpy-faced, but you are sitting there with a 'cat ate canary' grin."

His dark eyes flickered up to mine. "You are what you eat."

Now, it was my turn to blush. Dirty innuendos. Dear god. All I wanted to do was take him into the house where it was warm and see how far that teasing could go.

"Okay, if there is no chance of me getting you out of those pants, you are going to have to chill out with the dirty jokes. Pervy puns are the best way to get me naked."

He grinned, and I could see amusement dance in his eyes. "Forgive me, but your magic is...potent."

"I don't even know what that means." I remembered the way the magic had spilled out of me and into him, the way life had poured into him. I couldn't quite resist the urge to reach out and touch his cheek. "Holy crap, you are alive. You are breathing."

He nodded. "I am; my blood...flows."

I did not look down. Ohhh, I wanted to. But I don't think my very loose relationship with control could handle knowing that he was still ready for more. "Dude."

He stood up and bowed. "Forgive me, Lorena; it has been many, many years since I have felt life in my veins, and your life is tinged with magic."

I remembered what Zane had told me about the dietary preferences of vampires. "Do you like witches?"

He raised one brow. "In particular? No. I have no great preference for a particular taste of blood. At least, I didn't think I did." He eyed my neck with naked hunger, and all I could do was think about what else ought to be naked. I clapped a hand over my wound.

"Dude...yes or no?"

"Hmm?"

"You are telling me no, but you keep making jokes and telling me about your blood flow. Be honest...yes or no?"

He thought about it. I could see the thoughts flying over his face. The raw desire followed by aching need followed by that streak of stubbornness that I knew too well.

"No," he finally said, sounding more like Wei than he had in the past few minutes, "no, I cannot. I will not. I'm sorry, Lorena. I should not have...teased. Your blood is like a heady wine, and it made me forget myself. It made me remember a me that has long been dead. I cannot have you. I will not have you. It would only end in heartache."

Before I could argue, he turned into mist and vanished into the softening night.

"Damnit!" I cursed, stomping one foot against the cold ground. I was mad. I was so damn mad, and I wasn't sure why. So what if I didn't get any action from Wei the grumpy vampire? Okay, Wei the usually grumpy, weirdly complicated, sometimes funny vampire. Who cared? I still had Zane, and if Zane decided that me fooling around with Wei was a deal breaker, which I would totally understand, then there were still Alan and Dmitri. I could get action.

Yeah. Sure, I could.

I stomped inside and went immediately to a mirror. A large bruise was on my neck. It was the same dark blue as a midnight sky, but there was a softness around the edges that told me it would heal. With a snarl, I poured some antiseptic on it--who knew where that boy's mouth had been? -- and then slapped a Band-Aid on it. Good enough.

Then, knowing that I had lost a pretty decent amount of blood, I went to the kitchen and made myself a glass of juice, which I finished in three long gulps, and a sandwich. I poured myself another glass of juice and plopped down at the kitchen table.

Screw Wei. No, I amended, no screwing Wei. That was half of my problem. I took a large bite of my sandwich and grumped privately. I did my best not to think about that smile, the dance in his eyes, the dirty jokes. Man, who knew that all of that was hiding beneath that perfectly frigid mask? Well, point of fact, I did. I had known there was more dancing beneath all that veneer. I'd just ignored it because he hadn't wanted to show it.

I liked that guy. I liked that glimmer that I had seen of the man that he had been. I also liked when he was hiding it all away behind that cool emotionlessness mask, probably because I knew how deep that still ocean seemed to go.

Oh crap, I thought. I liked him. I really liked him. Not just his body, but everything else. I liked his stupid complications, and I liked the way he tried to hide himself because he was afraid of feeling too much. I liked the way he could go from hot to cold and back again with just a few words from me. I liked that he made me feel the same things. I liked that he was my mirror, opposite and similar all at once.

"Crap." I tossed down my sandwich. I was falling in love, and I really didn't have time for that. "Crap." I said again with more emphasis.

I heard a car pull up, and I turned to look out the window. A moment later, Jenny and Reikah came towards the front door. They weren't paying any attention to me. Instead, their fingers were laced together, pale brown and darker brown, one set of nails perfectly manicured, the other completely lacking in paint or lacquer. Their giggles were bright, cheerful, and soft.

They paused on the doorstep, but the door itself was thin enough that I could hear their conversation.

"Thank you," Reikah said, a little breathlessly.

"For what?" Jenny asked.

"For listening to me, for not...pushing. For just accepting me."

"I like you, Reikah. I don't know why, since you drive me nuts, but if you need to figure yourself out, take all the time you need to do that. You want to snuggle and hold hands and dance outside the school until four in the morning? That's great. That's all I need."

"Promise?"

"I swear."

There was a long silence, and I turned my head to peek out the window, feeling like a terrible person but not terrible enough to stop myself. They were standing in the moonlight, oblivious to the cold, their foreheads pushed gently together. If I had a camera, I would have taken a picture; they looked that beautiful.

"Will...will you kiss me goodnight?"

Jenny's eyes flicked open. I could almost feel the hope from here. "Are you sure?" she asked.

"I've never been kissed. I'd like to...from you."

Jenny's grin was a mile wide. "You want me to give you your first kiss?"

"Please?"

Jenny didn't say anything else. She dropped Reikah's hand and tilted her head. I looked away. I could be a little bit of a voyeur, but I had to draw the line somewhere. I steadfastly focused on my sandwich and silently rooted for them. Here was hoping their relationship could work out because, as far as I could tell, all of mine were headed down the garbage disposal.

A few moments later, I heard the car again, and Reikah came inside. She didn't notice me; there were stars in her eyes and her makeup had long since faded. She looked lovely.

Unable to resist, I cleared my throat loud enough to make her jump. "Young lady," I said, doing my best mother hen imitation, "you had me and your father worried all night."

She gave me an embarrassed look that bordered on mortified. "Have you been awake all night?"

"No," I said honestly, "but clearly you have." I used my foot to push out one of the other chairs. "Details. Give them."

"Are you serious?"

"One hundred percent."

She eyed me. "Is there another sandwich?"

I smirked and tore mine in half, offering her that. She took it and then opened a bag of chips. "You went to the grocery store?"

"Zane took me. He says I need to eat better."

"He's right."

"He says I need to sleep better too, but that's not happening." I took another bite and added a handful of ranch-flavored Doritos to my plate. They weren't super healthy, but I didn't care. Ranch Doritos for the win. "Tell me everything."

She did. She told me about the pageant, the songs, the dinner, and how after everyone went home, a few of the teenagers gathered in the parking lot and turned on their cars to dance together and laugh.

"She was so much fun; I had an amazing time," Reikah said, pushing her now empty plate away from her. I stood up and gave both plates a rinse off, and started to do the other dishes while I was there.

"I'm glad."

"She kissed me goodnight."

"Oh?" I said, feigning ignorance. "How did you feel about that?"

She shrugged, but there was a blush on her cheeks. "I don't know. Complicated."

I nodded. "That's okay. You don't need to have it all figured out right now. Jenny's awesome. She'll wait for you."

"How did your date with Zane go?"

I shrugged. "Well, I promised him that he was the one I'd fulfill the prophecy with, but when Wei showed up after I woke up from a bad dream, I had a martial-arts-infused make-out session with him, so I'm going to file it all under the 'it's complicated' subheading and hope for the best."

"It sounds as if you have things to figure out too."

"Truth." A thought hit me, and I perked up. "Hey, what do you know about Somniamancy?"

"Dream magic?" She frowned. "That's Markus' brand of magic."

And just like that, a puzzle piece fell into place. My mind began to race. "Markus? You mean Creepy Dude? My mom's boyfriend slash, the leader of the Order slash, my sister's father? That Markus? He does dream magic?"

"Yes."

I frowned. "Wait, I thought he was dead. I was almost sure of it. When we left the compound...he was...well, he was really hurt."

I was having trouble remembering all the ins and outs; memory was weird that way. We had all gotten into this great big fight, and I remember Wei stabbing him in the side with a blade. I mean, as far as killing blows go, getting blooded by the sword of a three-hundred-and-forty-four-year-old vampire was pretty permanent, right?

I'd read enough comics to know better.

"Dangit, he's not dead, is he?"

She shook her head. "It's not likely. Not only is Markus very gifted with magic, but there are several healers in the Order. They would not have let him die."

"Yeah, cults are fanatical that way."

I sighed and put my chin on the table. "I was reading my grandmother's grimoire today. I think he's been attacking me with my dreams. They've been weird, and my sleep is all messed up."

Reikah shook her head. "That's not easy to do. He would need a connection with you."

"How could he make a connection?"

She thought that over. "He would have to be touching you for one. He could make a poppet of you, but as a witch, you are not as prone to that as a normal human. Or you'd have to be exposed to his connective sigils. Those could do it."

It all hit me like a brick. "Connective sigils!"

She blinked at me. "What?"

"I thought...oh god...I'm so stupid..." I pulled my phone out of my pocket, a little surprised that it wasn't broken or anything, and scrolled through my old messages. Then, I paused. "Can you look at the sigils and not be harmed?"

"If they are sigils meant for you, they will do nothing to me."

I showed her, and all I needed to see was her face paling. "Oh, Lorena...these are very powerful. How...when..."

"I've been getting them for a while. But that doesn't make sense. I got the first weird dream before the first message was sent."

She shook her head. "He could have been dream walking the first time, looking to get information about you. Scare you. After that..." she shrugged. "We need to do something."

"What do we need to do?"

She thought about it. "There are few ways to keep a Somniamancer out of your dreams. You'll need sigils and herbs..."

"Yeah, I read about those..." I brought out my grandmother's grimoire and showed her the page that I had marked. "Here."

She nodded. "Those are good starts, but we will need more. I'll need time, but I can add to these, personalize them, and make them more powerful. I'm quite good with sigils."

I thought back to the black paper lesson. Yeah, she was better with them than I was. "Okay, so when do we start?"

"Tonight. I need time to rest and prepare. I'm sorry it can't be sooner, but, Lorena, you cannot fall asleep. If this has been going on for as long as you say, he is stealing parts of your essence every time you rest. There may come a time when you do not wake up." She sounded legitimately scared.

"It's fine. I've got coffee and Netflix. I can stay up for days.

She frowned. "Perhaps I should call Jenny."

I shook my head. "Please don't. She's got to work, and she just had an amazing date. Please don't scare her with this. It won't help anything, not really.

I could tell that Reikah wanted to argue, but ultimately, she nodded. "If you insist. But please, stay awake, whatever you have to do.

"I'll enlist Maahes's help."

She frowned. "Ahh, yes, cats. They know everything about staying awake"

She had me there, but what could I do? I sent her off to bed for rest and settled down with my laptop and the largest cup of coffee I could manage. It was a great plan, I thought; it was too bad that everything was about to go crazy.

CHAPTER TEN

Staying awake all day was not what I would call an easy task, especially considering all the sleep I hadn't been having. However, I was surprised by what I could manage when the option of sleep was removed from my day.

My Netflix binge did not go as anticipated. Who would have known that sitting on the couch with a cat by my side while watching the new Voltron wasn't exactly an equation for wakefulness? When I nearly nodded off for the second time, I decided to get up and do something that had been nagging at me for weeks.

I was home. This place, small and simple as it was, was mine now, and I needed to really make that happen. I liked seeing my grandmother's knickknacks everywhere, and her books, and all of that...but they weren't mine.

So I started cleaning. I started with the shelves first. There were plenty of novels there, cute books, but not really my style. I put them in a box and set them to the side, replacing them with my own comic books, fantasy and science fiction novels, and even my very modest collection of Manga, all from team Clamp. They took up one shelf, but already I felt a little better.

I turned my attention to the big trunk that was also the living room table with a patchwork doily over the top. Inside was a huge collection of family photos, which I took a little too much time to look through.

I decided to leave those mostly alone. They were, after all, links to my own past. I was resituating everything when a letter fell out of one of the albums. I was just going to tuck it back in when I saw my name written on the front of the letter in my grandmother's handwriting.

The paper was soft beneath my fingers, as if it had been handled many times before. My fingers shook, and I had to put it down out of fear of ripping the aged paper when I unfolded it. My grandmother had written to me. The shock of it left me feeling a little lightheaded, though that might have been the four cups of extra strength coffee and the lack of sleep. What could she have had to say? Well, there was only one way to find out.

With a deep breath, I sat down on the floor, tucking my back against the couch, and ran my hands down my thighs to stop the shaking. Okay, stopping wasn't going to happen considering the coffee, but easing the shaking was.

I flexed my fingers and then picked up the letter. Yup, that was definitely my grandmother's handwriting. Between her journals and her grimoire, I knew the script well. And that was definitely my name scrawled carefully over the long flat plane. I cleared my throat and fixed my hair as if I was somehow going to make some kind of impression on a woman who had been dead for a while now.

"Just open the thing," I grumped at myself.

Carefully, I unfolded it. I read the contents, and then I read them again. It wasn't until the third time that I fully grasped everything that had been said.

My Dearest Lorena,

I am so sorry that I will never meet you. By the time you find this letter, you will know enough about me to understand how I know that you and I will never share the memories that a grandmother ought to share with her granddaughter. I hope you know that I regret not having a place in your life while I am alive, more than anything else.

There is a part of me that hates having told your father about the prophecy. Maybe then I could have helped you grow into the woman who took part in bringing magic into the world. That was my own hubris that couldn't believe that my own child might react how he did. Then again, it is my son we are talking about. My son, for all he was a smart boy, could be foolish when it came to girls. When he brought that wizard girl home, I thought he had just about lost his mind, but I remember how my mother reacted when I told her that Jake was going to be my husband. I had promised that I wasn't going to do the same.

I'm rambling. I'm sorry. I can't help myself. There is so much to tell you and I honestly do not know how much time left there is. Isn't that strange? A Seer who doesn't know when she will die. Well, I am sure it won't be long now.

Let me start at the beginning.

My son brought home your mother, and he told me that she was pregnant. They were young, no older than you are now, and still fumbling around in the world. Even so, I was shocked. Your father, out of foolishness or rebellion, had taken up with a wizard girl. I do not like to think of myself as a bigot, but their way of looking at magic has always left a sour taste in my mouth. Even so, I secretly hoped that she would reawaken his love of magic, a thing he had given up shortly before he grew into a man.

They asked for help. They asked for a place to stay. I couldn't deny them. For all the girl was a little odd, he was my child and she was going to be giving birth to my grandchild. I wasn't going to turn them away now. I took them into my home. I had hoped that your mother would grow on me. I am ashamed to say she didn't.

Oh, she was a girl, the kind of girl that no matter how old she got, she'd never be a woman. One moment she was batting her eyes at my son, and the next she was snapping at me and then weeping about it all. For a while, I told myself that it was the hormones that come with being pregnant, but after a while, I knew better. The girl was a manipulative little hen, and I wanted little to do with her.

When she declared that she was pregnant with twins, my son was overjoyed. I was not. After all, I had already seen that my son would only have one child. How could there be two? Well, I figured that out well enough as well. There were two children in her belly alright, but only one of them belonged to my boy. When I talked to her about it, she threw a fit, a grand one if I do say so myself, and told me that my witchcraft wasn't perfect. That it was a lesser form of magical casting.

Oh, it took everything in me not to slap that little sneer off of her face. But I managed. My son, for reasons I could not understand, loved her, and at least one of those babies was my grandchild. She would have to do a great deal more to make me forget myself enough to lash out.

That moment, however, did come.

It was just before you were born. A week or two at best. I saw the prophecy. Oh, Lorena, my dear granddaughter. I saw what would happen. I saw the prophecy that was laid before you. It shook me. I don't know if I was scared for you or excited for what might happen. Looking back now, I think it was both.

I told your father. I told him everything that I had seen. I don't know what I expected of him. A part of me still hoped that he would remember who and what he was. That he was a witch, he was a Quinn. What a fool I was to see that he was angry at me. He called me names. Told me that his daughter was going to be normal. She was going to go to school. She was going to have friends. No one was going to make fun of her or be afraid of her.

Then, he asked about his other child, and I was so angry with him that I blurted out that he had no other child. That his little wizard had played him false. That she had been going around with someone else. He looked shattered. I hated myself a little for taking the light out of his eyes.

Oh, Lorena, it was then I knew.

I asked him to turn around. It took a good deal of convincing, but I managed. There, on his back, I found it. It was a wizardry. A circle of magic inscribed on his back. A love spell. Of all the terrible things. A love spell!

I do not know how much you have read into your studies, but love spells, and many spells of compulsion, are against the rules. It is one thing to bless a woman to have children, but it is another thing entirely to force a man to participate.

I think, somehow, your mother must have known something. How she knew that my son's child would be special I don't know, but I am convinced she did. After all, when I helped remove the symbol, we both realized that she didn't care two wits for him. It became even clearer when he confronted her. How it all would have turned out I don't know because the little twit chose just that moment to give birth.

What a night that was, Lorena. What a night!

Before it was all over, my son was already wrapping you up and packing. He said he needed to get as far away from this mountain and the women on it as he could. I begged him to stay, pleaded with him. Told him that his daughter, that you, were going to be special. He said that you were special, just not in the way that I saw. He let me take one picture with you, one memento for me to keep.

While we were fighting over you, that little wizard absconded with her other child. Where they went I don't know. I don't care to know. I only hope that little girl she gave birth to is alright.

So there you have it. How everything happened. I hope it answers some of your questions because now I have to tell you more.

I have Seen so much about you, Lorena. I have watched you grow up from the distant eye of a Seer. Every night, I go to sleep and I hope that I will See a little more about you. I know that you are creative and imaginative and a little stubborn. I know that you have grown up beautifully, if a little lonely. I know too that, when you get here, you will step into a world that you will fall in love with, and I am so happy for that.

What I also know, Lorena, is that you cannot trust everyone in your life. I wish I could tell you more, but my visions, especially as I grow older, do not come in as clear as they once did.

Someone, my dear, someone in your life is manipulating you, and I cannot tell you who. I am so sorry that I cannot offer you more than that. I have tried every tea and mixture and tonic I can think of to help clear up this vision. All I know is that you must be careful when you walk in dreams. I hope that helps you.

Be safe, my dear. Know that I love you and that I am here in every way I can be.

Blessings,

Loretta Quinn

P.S. Take care of Maahes. He looks forward to meeting you.

I put the letter down. There were tears on my cheeks. Weirdly enough, the shaking hadn't stopped. Funny how that kind of stuff happens when you've pretty much been told that at least one of the people that you trusted couldn't be trusted.

Maybe she was wrong. That was the first thing I told myself. Maybe my grandmother had been wrong about everything. Maybe I wasn't a prophecy girl. I was just plain ol' Lorena Quinn. I was not special. I was just here. I was just going to live my life, and nothing magical was happening, and I could trust everyone around me.

Yeah. Sure. And pigs with wings were going to fly out of my nose, and Bruce Wayne was going to make me the next Robin. Uh-huh.

I couldn't stop myself from making up a mental list of the people that I did trust. It wasn't a long list. There was Alan, the pretty vampire. I hadn't heard all that much from him since I moved out of the mansion. The same could be said for Dmitri. I trusted them. Okay, I trusted Alan more. Dmitri scared me a little. Then there was Wei. I wholeheartedly trusted Wei. Should I? He was so complicated. Maybe I couldn't.

I shook my head, but the thoughts I didn't want kept coming.

Jenny, Zane, Reikah. I trusted them too. Maybe I shouldn't. Maybe I couldn't How was I supposed to know?

I tossed down the letter and began to pace the length of the living room. Who did she mean? Why did her seeing ability have to get all wonky later in life? Ugh! Okay, no, that wasn't fair. She didn't have any control over that, and I certainly wasn't going to spend the next who knew how long, blaming a dead woman for not giving perfect advice.

What I was going to do was prepare myself. I really wished I could do one of those nifty neato montages that they did in action flicks where I just got better over the next twenty minutes while "Eye of the Tiger" played in the background.

Since that wasn't going to happen, I decided to do the next best thing. I took a brief inventory of what I did know how to do.

In the past few weeks, I had learned how to tug at ley lines, talk to ghost cats, and play with the elements. I could create a wizard's circle...usually, and I could multiply my magic when a vampire bit me.

It was not a very impressive amount of skills.

"Well done, Lorena. You were so focused on dating that you pretty much forgot that you were supposed to be practicing magic. Just had to get that job, didn't you?"

I shook my head and blew out a breath. Getting frustrated with myself wasn't going to help anything. Time to think.

Dreams. My grandmother had mentioned dreams, and someone was attacking me with dreams. That someone was probably Markus, but until I knew for sure, I wasn't going to make too many assumptions. I'd read enough plot twists to know better.

I pulled out my grandmother's grimoire and read everything that there was to know about dreams and dream magic. When that was done, I focused my research on protecting myself and keeping my astral self, my dream self, connected to my body.

It was the best that I could do.

"Afternoon," Reikah said sleepily, coming out of the back room of my grandmother's house. "You ready?"

"Can I trust you?" I blurted, because I was Queen of smooth social interaction.

"Huh?" she asked, rubbing sleep out of her eyes. "Yes? With what?"

"Like, overall. Can I trust you? Why aren't you with the Order anymore? You still like the way they do magic?"

She gave me a look, but the sleep was slowly coming out of her eyes. "What?"

"I realized that I've never actually asked you why you wanted to leave your little hermit order. It's not because you don't agree with the way they practice magic, since you still talk the way they do. I guess I'm just confused."

Reikah narrowed her eyes. "You want to know why I helped you leave?"

"Yeah, I guess that's part of it."

She sighed and sat down on the other side of the kitchen table, still cluttered with all the notes I had tried to cram in the past few hours.

"I do believe that magic ought to be practiced with regularity. I believe that sigils, circles, and symbols are important. I think that a person should be careful when utilizing magic. Considering the lethal ability of magic, I don't think that is a bad thing to believe."

I sat back, crossing my arms over my chest. "You think witchcraft is inferior."

She sighed. "Inferior isn't the right word. If you wish to use a comparison, it is the difference between using a firecracker to remove a stump, or a tractor. Both can do the job, but a firecracker can cause a great deal of damage."

"So can a tractor."

She nodded. "Yes. But even so. Even if I believed that witchcraft was inferior to wizardry, even if I thought that you shouldn't fulfill the prophecy, I think hurting other people to make that happen is wrong."

I wanted to believe her. With a sigh, I dragged my hand down my face and told her about the letter.

"You are worried that I have been living with you, secretly still working with The Order?"

"It's stupid."

"No, it's logical. I commend you. Of all the people who could be against you, I am certainly the most obvious choice."

I don't know why her agreeing with me made me feel worse, but it did. "Okay, well, until I know better, I'm going to trust you."

"Well that's foolish."

I shrugged. "My grandmother said my dad is foolish, so I guess I take after him."

She gave me a look of complete exasperation. "If you aren't sure you can trust me, you ought to do this dream walking thing yourself."

I nodded. I probably should, but I just didn't know enough. Instead, I reached across the table and took her hand. "A few weeks ago, Connie was my friend. I would have done anything she asked of me short of committing murder. I screwed up there, and I know better now, but I'm not going to let that experience and a letter from a dead woman make me go crazy with who I can and can't trust."

I thought I saw a smile, but she quickly hid it. "Still foolish."

I shrugged. It was true. "Okay, so tell me how this is going to work."

She went over it; then, she went over it again. She was going over it a third time, with my help, when Alan crashed through the door.

"Where is Wei?"

I blinked. I had never seen Alan look so scared. In fact, I had never seen Alan look anything but mildly amused at everything.

"What do you mean?" I demanded. My heart had gone from zero to a hundred and eighty in less than two seconds. "What happened?"

"Wei did not return last night."

I felt lightheaded. My vision swam in front of my eyes. I am pretty sure I would have fallen to the floor were it not for someone catching me. When I felt velvet and lace against my cheek, I knew that it was Alan.

"What?" I whispered. Maybe I had heard him wrong. Yeah. That was it. I wasn't living in denial at all. "What do you mean he didn't return?"

"He went to guard you." Alan placed me gently back on the chair.

I raised my eyebrow. "Guard me?"

"We've been taking turns guarding you, watching over you. It was for your safety. But Wei did not return."

That was news, and none of it good.

"Oh my god," I whispered. I felt like I was beginning to understand something. An idea was pushing in the back of my head. "But Zane was here for some of the night."

Alan frowned. "Zane? Why was he here?"

I blushed. I assumed that Alan and Dmitri would have been informed. "I...I may have told him that I was going to fulfill the prophecy with him." Man, it was a really good way of saying sleeping together. Far less embarrassing...yeah.

Alan's eyebrows flicked up. "Why?"

The blush went from rose to tomato. "I don't know; maybe because I was told he was the best option?"

Alan frowned at me. "I thought love was the most important thing to you."

"Do you really want a play-by-play of how I ended up making this decision? Because that does not seem like the most important thing here."

Alan placed a hand on my shoulder. "Zane did not return last night either."

I felt my heart skip a beat. "Oh god."

Zane. Zane was the one I couldn't trust. Wasn't he? He was probably still in love with Connie. Maybe he had never wanted to leave the Order.

"But why would he agree to be my partner if he's bad?" I asked out loud. "What about all the dreams? It doesn't make any sense. It's just flat out confusing."

"Lorena?" Reikah took my hand. "What do you want to do?"

I wanted to go find Wei, but I was so tired. I had thought skipping a night of sleep or two once in a while was no big deal, but I was quickly growing aware of the effect that too much caffeination and not enough rest was having. My head was aching, my body was shaking, and I knew that there was no way I was going to be of help to anyone until I got sleep.

"Alan, you and Dmitri need to go looking for Wei, and Zane too. I think if we find one, we will find the other. Maybe Zane is the bad guy, maybe he's a victim. I don't know. Find at least one of them. Send Jenny over here. Tell her we are doing magic."

Alan smiled at me. "Taking this prophecy woman thing seriously, aren't you?"

I wanted to smile back, but I just couldn't. Not with Wei gone. The fact that I was more worried about Wei than Zane was not lost on me.

"Find Wei," I said.

Alan placed a kiss on my forehead. "I will."

I watched him go as quickly as he had come in and turned my focus back on Reikah. "Okay, lucid dreaming, that's what the sigils are?"

She cleared her throat. For a moment, she just looked at me as if to make sure that I was serious. It was a good thing that I had never been more serious about anything in my entire life. Yeah, Wei was missing, and so was Zane. There was a chance that something absolutely terrible had happened to them. Yeah, that was totally a thing. But the fact was I could not worry about it right now since some dream mage person was trying to kill me with my sleep. I mean, don't get me wrong; dying in my sleep was the preferred way to go, but not when I couldn't even legally drink. So, I had to compartmentalize.

Checklist:
Review sigil magic
Use dream magic to fight Somniamancer
Rest
Find vampire make-out buddy
Save world

Seemed like an average day in my life.

"Lucid dreaming is a stage of dreaming where you realize you are dreaming and can still be asleep," I prompted, encouraging Reikah to trust me. It worked.

"Yes, the sigils that I am making for you will help you dream lucidly. The way that most Somniamancers achieve victory is by making you forget that you are dreaming, so that when they hurt you, the damage is permanent because your mind believes it so fully. We are going to give you that boost. The sachets you made will help, but we are going to work some protective magics in too.

I nodded. "Okay, let's do this."

"Now?" she asked, looking shocked.

"Would you like to wait a week?"

"Well...yes," she admitted, "I don't think we are ready."

I spread my hands wide. "Clark Kent wasn't ready for Zod, but he made it work."

"Your comparisons confuse me."

"Please, being a nerd is status quo. Let's do this."

A few minutes later, Reikah was dipping a fine-tipped brush into a pot of dark blue ink. I was laying on my grandmother's bed. Maahes had curled up at the top of my head like some sort of protective kitty hat, and half of me was painted with complicated symbols that I truly didn't understand. I really hoped I could trust Reikah.

Every time the brush hit my skin, I felt another tingle of magic. I remembered what my grandmother had said about my father, about the love spell that had been imprinted on his skin and he hadn't even known.

"Hey, Reikah?" I asked.

"Hmm?"

"You'll be able to wake me up, right?"

She looked down at me with those big serious eyes. "When you are ready, you'll be able to wake up all on your own."

I hoped she was right, because it was getting harder and harder to stay awake. My eyelids were heavy. Maybe if I just rested for a little while…I'd be okay, right? Yeah. Just a little rest.

When I opened my eyes again, it was morning.

THE FINAL CHAPTER

The morning was clear and bright, and a breeze was coming in through my window. The lacy curtains that I seriously needed to switch out for something a little more me were fluttering softly with it. A layer of snow had covered the ground, but with a breeze like that, it wasn't going to last for very long.

I rolled over in bed, and there was Wei. Even with his back to me, I knew who he was. The long line of dark hair was loose rather than braided, and it made a blanked over his shoulders. Even so, there was just enough of that golden skin showing through.

"Wei!" I gasped. "You are alright!"

He shifted slowly and rolled over; the blanket slid down just far enough that I was pretty sure that he was naked. I had to swallow pretty hard. Wei wasn't like Alan, prone to wearing clothes unbuttoned to his naval, but I'd seen him topless once or twice, and it never failed to leave me a little breathless. All of those sleek muscles shifted and bunched as he stretched out against the bed and offered me a tiny smile.

"I was waiting for you to wake up," he said, reaching a hand out for me. I took it. I couldn't help myself. I was so happy to see him. I pressed his palm to my cheek and gave his palm a soft kiss.

"Alan said you were gone."

"I'm not gone; I'm here."

He sat up, and the blanket slipped lower. Yup. Definitely naked. I was going to slide out of the bed when he pulled me suddenly into his lap. My hand landed on a scar on his side. I don't remember Wei having a scar there. What had happened? I wanted to ask him, but the devastating smile he shot in my direction had the thought melting right out of my head.

"I could prove to you how very here I am."

I let out the most god-awful laugh. A regular girl would have giggled lightly, maybe even offered some seductive and witty repartee. Me? I made a sound like a whimpering puppy and a sick donkey. Yeah, there is a reason I've never gone all the way with a guy before, and that reason is total awkwardness.

But he smiled and kissed me anyway, and the next thing I knew, my back was against the bed. He kissed me, and I enjoyed it. No, 'enjoy' isn't the word. The word for how much I liked it probably isn't PG-13. Heck, it probably isn't even rated R.

"Wei," I said, pulling him closer.

He kissed slowly down my neck and then further. He didn't answer.

"Wei, are we really going to do this? I don't think I am ready for another round of blue ovaries."

He didn't answer, and that bothered me. Wei always answered me. Even in the middle of a make-out session, Wei was a responsive kind of person. Sometimes too responsive. Also, wasn't this about the time that he hauled out on me?

"Wait," I said, pushing at his shoulder, "I don't feel right."

Wei lifted his head, but it's wasn't Wei's face staring back at me. It was Zane's. Then, it was Alan's. Then, it was Dmitri's.

Dreaming. I was dreaming. Crap. This wasn't real. This wasn't real at all. I pulled back from the hot male body draped over me and scampered back. "Oh no no no no no."

"What's wrong?" a voice asked. I knew the voice, but I couldn't place it. I wasn't sure why. My head felt weird.

Another breeze came in the window, and it was a very cold breeze.

"Get away from me!" I snapped.

I scrambled more. I really wanted to get off the bed, but it was like the mattress never ended.

"Lorena? What's wrong? I thought you wanted to be with me."

If I hadn't been sure that the shape changing body over me wasn't Wei, that line right there would have sealed the deal. Wei wouldn't say that. He'd say something about me being confusing or he'd bow politely and offer some kind of apology. The man on the bed was not Wei, and I was guessing he wasn't any of the vampire guys.

"Show your face, Markus, you creep."

The smile on Wei's face stretched strangely. It was another man's smile on top of Wei's features. I did not like it. It was creepy, and I really wanted it to go away.

"Crafty little witch."

"Unprepared creepy wizard."

The image of Wei flickered and then disappeared entirely. There was Markus, Mr. Average Height and Average Build himself. Markus was the kind of middle aged guy that they'd get to stand in for the dad character in those photographs they put inside picture frames. The kind where they say 'look at this attractive happy family; this could be you.'

What I'm saying is he was so average-perfect that he creeped me out. It didn't help that he had just been having a dream make-out session with me while wearing my maybe-boyfriend's face. Yeah, extra creepy.

"There's no need to act like that, Lorena. We can be friends."

"Dude, friends don't trap friends inside creepy dreams while slowly milking all their energy. Just sayin'."

He almost smiled. "You look so like your mother."

Okay, ew. Gross. I was not okay with this. Not even a little bit, not even at all. "Okay, creepy step-father, let me the hell out of this dreamscape. Right now."

He chuckled. "Why would you want to go back? Why do you want to go live in a tiny house with people who are too involved in what is going on with themselves to give you what you need?"

"What the heck are you talking about?"

"Well, what do you think is going to happen when Jenny and the little traitor get on with their lives? Right now, all three of you can hang out, but you know what happens to the third wheel even in the average relationship. But those two, who are just beginning to live openly? They are going to forget you; after all, they'll want to hang out with other women who date women. They don't want to be seen with a girl who surrounds herself with men."

"That's a lie. Jenny and Reikah are my friends. It doesn't matter if they are dating or not."

He tsked and stretched. The white sheet he had been wearing slithered around him to create a pretty impressive toga. I was happy that he was wearing clothes, but I'd much rather he wasn't here at all.

"And once you choose a vampire, the rest will ignore you. After all, they haven't spent much time with you after Zane stepped in, have they?"

I blinked. I didn't want to agree with that, but he wasn't totally wrong. Wei had showed up, but apparently only because he was guarding me, not because he actually wanted to be with me.

"They-well-I..." I stammered, unable to put together a full sentence.

He tsked again, and the bed seemed to disappear. For a moment, I was falling into a great white nothingness, my pajamas fluttering around my body. I could feel that weightless feeling in my belly, and I gotta admit that I was in no way a fan.

I really wished I was Supergirl or Wonder Woman. Supergirl could fly, and Wonder Woman had an invisible jet and, barring that, could jump really well. Yeah, I really would rather be Wonder Woman; she was cool.

Wait a minute. This was my dream. I'd been Diana, Princess of Themyscira before. I'd had some pretty epic dream battles and made out with one of several versions of Clark Kent. Why not now?

The next thing I knew, I was wearing the outfit. I don't mean the new dark DC universe one; I mean the old school one piece bathing suit style with the star spangled underoos and the red and gold top. I had a sword on one hip, a lasso on the other and I could fly.

Wonder Woman couldn't, but this was my dream, dangit; if I wanted to be Wonder Woman and fly, I was going to do it.

And while we were thinking about Paradise Island…

The world shifted beneath me, and suddenly, Markus and I were standing on a beach. I could smell the salty air whip my ash brown curls around the golden tiara that sat on my forehead. He did not look happy with me.

"How did you do that?" he demanded.

"Dude, this is my head. You wanna screw around with my dreams, you are going to have to get on my level."

He snarled and shifted. At first, I thought he was going to be a dog, maybe even the creepy dog with the sharp teeth that followed my half-sister around. Then, he grew to be roughly the size of my grandmother's house, and added a couple of heads. His fur was black as pitch and his eyes like cheap rubies. I didn't need all those comics to recognize Cerberus.

"You wanna play this way? You could let me go."

His response was a trio of howls that reverberated in the ears.

"Okay."

There was a part of me that knew it would come to this. That I would have to fight him. That it was only going to be one of us leaving this dream. I really wanted it to be me.

I launched myself at him, my own battle scream pouring out of my throat. It was much better than my attempt at a giggle, probably because I was actually fearing for my life.

I don't know if it was all the comics I had read, my martial arts training, or the fact that this was a dream, but I moved really fast and I struck really hard. My sword disappeared into his side, but there was no blood, just a shadowy sort of smoke.

"That's not fair," I said, slamming my sword in again.

One of the heads dipped and snapped around my middle; he shook me hard, hard enough that I saw spots behind my eyes. When my vision was going gray, I was pretty sure I saw Jenny and Reikah staring down at me, but when I blinked, they were gone.

"Okay, no more nice girl."

The three-headed beast tossed his head as I whirled on him. The dreamscape had changed yet again. Rather than a glorious sun-swept island with crystalline sand beaches and water like liquid sapphires, I was in a layer of hell. Or, I thought as I looked at the massive three-headed dog, more like a section of Hades.

It was like some big underground cave with a hundred stalactites and stalagmites interrupting a clear line of sight. Small basins of boiling hot water pushed thick clouds of steam into the air, causing yet another problem for my vision. The steam collected in big pockets of the rock ceiling, and then dripped down to collect on the floor. My bright red boots, while totally stylish, were traitorously slick.

Damn.

I tried to change my outfit again. It resisted, or rather the dream did. In my own place, the surrealistic version of my grandmother's bedroom, everything had been as easy to sculpt as wet clay. Here and now, it was like chiseling away at marble: possible, but harder to do.

"I won't let you escape," a strange trio of voices called out through the murky dark.

"You watch too many bad movies," I snapped back.

"You want to unleash magic."

I sighed. Hadn't I already had this conversation before? Pretty sure I had. "Listen, why don't you ask your girlfriend, or even your daughter, about my views on that? Okay?"

After finally managing to give myself some sensible shoes in this god forsaken dreamscape, I began trying to navigate through the hellish dimension. Even with my new shoes, every step was traitorous. I kept my sword in one hand and a shield in the other, lasso bouncing on my hip. Dressing up as my favorite super hero was nice and all, but I wasn't sure how much help it was going to be. Why had my sword just gone through the beast like it was made out of smoke?

"If I could wake up, I would."

That had me stopping in my path.

"Wait, what?"

I shifted my body between two pieces of rock, watching as the massive beast swayed back and forth in what looked like a large cavern. The black fur was slick with the humid heat of the cave.

"Don't you remember what your little boyfriend did?"

Wei was neither little nor my boyfriend, but it seemed kind of stupid to grump about that right that moment. Instead, I shifted my body in an effort to hide until I could figure out what I ought to do.

"I remember," he continued, clearly willing to go on a villainous rant about everything that was making him a bitter creep. That was fine. He could monologue all he wanted. I needed time to think. "In a misguided effort to rescue you from a comfortable custody, he and that little group of miscreants attacked me."

Man, did this dude take bad guy monologues one-oh-one? I was guessing so. Only mustache-twirling villains used words like miscreants. And what was this about comfortable custody? Pretty sure he meant forced isolation, or some other word for imprisonment, because that's exactly what had happened.

"We fought, and I would have had him if it weren't for you."

I couldn't help myself. "And you would have gotten away with it too if it weren't for us rotten kids."

His head snapped in my direction, all six bright red eyes narrowed at me. I went as absolutely still as I could imagine, wishing suddenly that I could turn to rock. Then, I felt the slow shift of magic, and when I was brave enough to open my eyes, my body had shifted to look like my surroundings.

Hmm, I thought to myself, *more Mystique than Wonder Woman, but I'd totally take it*. My sword and shield were gone, but if all I was going to do was sneak around and hide, I didn't need weapons. Besides, a sword hadn't done me a whole lot of good. But why? I thought that hurting a body in a dreamscape should have some kind of response. Then again, my grasp of dream magic was tenuous at best.

Okay, Lorena, think. I hunkered down behind another large rock and pieced together what I knew about my enemy and the world we were in.

Lucid dreaming was the short-lived time period between the point when a person was in the deep sleep where dreams happened, and the lighter sleep where they didn't. In this place, dreams were malleable, changeable. A practiced dream walker could stay in a lucid dream for a lot longer than the average person. They could even, with some skill, enter another person's dreams. Every entrance was easier than the one before it, and after a while, a dream walker could start to fiddle around with someone's dreams.

Somniamancers were especially good at it. Okay, fine. Markus, leader of the Order of the Loyal Hermit, was a Somniamancer. He could, with very little effort, create a dream world, or dreamscape, to trap a person in. *Like,* I thought as sweat dripped down my back, *you know, a Hades-infused dimension of humid-laden hell.* They could mess with a person's heads, and therefore bodies, with their particular brand of magic.

Something was niggling at me, though. He was pretty pissed about Wei stabbing him. I couldn't blame him for that. There weren't a whole lot of people who liked getting stabbed in the gut. But it had been a pretty lethal shot. How was Markus even alive?

My train of thought was interrupted as the shape of Cerberus swiped out suddenly. Its huge paws swept out, each head gnashed in a trio of directions. Even that long canine tail swept dangerously around, making a circle of carnage that barely missed me, but hit a whole lot of rock.

The world began to quake. My footing was even less sure as rock crumbled around me. I lunged and dodged as fast as I could, trying my best to think quick thoughts. The safest place, I decided, was closer to the beast.

I tumbled into the large egg-shaped cavern and beneath the massive paws of the dog.

"He stabbed me, while infused with your power." Cerberus snarled in Markus' voice.

Had he? I had to think about it. That part of my memory wasn't as clear. I remember pushing power into Zane to get him moving again. Then...oh right. I had. I had been so overwhelmed with my own budding power that I connected with all of the vampires. Alan, Dmitri, Zane, and Wei had been connected to me for just a moment. I managed to give them all a little boost against the evil villain.

"I can still feel it, your death magic, swimming in my veins."

Was that a thing? I didn't know. Heck, I knew pretty much jack about necromancy outside of what happened in video games. Necromancy was death magic, or at least the manipulation of life. It probably wasn't so comfortable to have it, as he said, swimming in the veins. Was that it, I wondered, was he hovering somewhere on the edge of death? Did that explain the smoke? Or how he always managed to be asleep when I was? Because it was a little weird that he was messing with pretty much all of my dreams. And maybe having my magic inside of him gave him some kind of link.

I didn't know, but it was all I had to work with.

The dog swung its heads this way and that, turning in a tight circle as if trying to zero in on something. Me, I assumed. I flattened myself against the ground and wondered exactly what I was going to do with my newfound knowledge.

"I must be rid of you."

I rolled my shoulders, and thought about that.

If my magic was inside of him, couldn't I do something about that? I had to. But what?

I didn't have the time to think about it as a large, black paw slammed down around me. I'd been hurt before, but it was nothing like this. Getting hit by a practice weapon, or falling on the cold hard ground after a practice session with Wei did not, in any way, compare to this all-over sensation of being crushed. The weight pushed the air out of my lungs, and then it kept pushing down. I was aware of my bones grinding against one another, the blood pumping through my body. He was squashing me like a grape, and I had absolutely no interest in being juice.

He ripped his paw suddenly to the side, and I flopped around like a rag doll. Claws, half as long as my forearm, swept across my body. It didn't matter that I looked like a rock; I certainly didn't feel like it. I was just flesh and blood and bone, and all of it was battered.

Blood puddled beneath me, sticky and hot. That couldn't be good, could it? Nope. Not at all.

He swiped me with the other paw, sending me flying across the floor, scraping up my shoulders, my face, my arm. I was in so much pain from everything else that I barely felt it. That did not strike me as a good sign. My vision was blurry, and my arms felt too heavy to move. I was pretty sure I was dying, and there was some distant part of me that was totally okay with that.

"Not yet," a voice, male and kind, whispered down at me. "You must fight, Lorena."

"Dad?" I asked.

"Shhhh. It's your dream. Take control."

Magic slithered through me, warm and familiar and smelling deeply of herbs. I felt better for it, more energized. I managed to sit up, coppery blood still clinging to my arms, but I could move them again. That was good.

"Why won't you die?"

With great effort, I lifted my head. I could still see the beast prowling towards me, but it was a shadow of itself, flickering around the image of a man. I didn't know Markus well enough to pick him out at the distance of a dream, but I made a leap of logic.

"You first," I snapped back.

I don't know when the Wonder Woman gear came back, but there it was, all blue and yellow and red. I dove at the beast, and knew in the way that you know in dreams, that he wasn't real. The only thing that was real in this whole blasted place was the man in the center of the creature. I dove for him, and when I got there, I slammed against a globe of protective magic, bouncing off of it with all the elegance of a bug against a windshield.

Hell disappeared, and we stood facing each other against a vast, empty nothingness. It was neither black nor white but a soft smoky gray. I wore my pajamas, and he was wearing what looked like a medical nightgown, the kind that had the ties to keep it shut in the back. He didn't look as unimposingly attractive as I had remembered; he looked withered. If I was a squashed grape, then he was a raisin. His skin was crumpled around his body. His eyes had large sagging dark circles around them, and the muscles that had been firm and fit just a few weeks ago were withered.

"What the heck happened?"

His eyes lit up with the frothing anger of the vengeful and obsessed. "You happened, you pathetic little witch! Your corruption."

"Well, that's a bit harsh." I responded.

"You did this!" He reached one hand out towards me Vader style, and I felt a surge of magic hit me. It was hard enough that I decided I would rather have been stepped on by a mythological dog all over again. "You infested me."

"I didn't mean to," I managed to say between fits of choking coughs. It was the truth, but even as I said it, I knew that it was a weak excuse. I hadn't meant to do this. I had only meant to get free. How was I supposed to know that it would twist him this way?

"You think that matters?" he snarled. His wrinkled face contorted monstrously. The lips were too wide, the eyes too large. Everything was just enough out of proportion to be unsettling. "What you meant to do doesn't matter. This is what you did. This is the corruption that will unleash itself on the world. Do you really think a woman filled with death can ever create life? You will bring nothing but desecration to this world."

I said the only thing I could. "I'm sorry."

He howled in rage. "I don't want your apology. I want your death."

He pounced on me then. Despite his decrepitude, he moved like a lash. He slammed into me, toppling me to the ground. Out of reflex, I used a martial arts move to send him flying past me. He wasn't deterred. He flung himself at me again. I didn't correct myself fast enough, and he slammed into me with all the power that hate and anger could give a person.

His fingers were like slender branches, twirling around my throat, growing ever tighter. I grabbed at them, ripped at them, but it didn't seem to matter. He shoved me against the unrelenting nothingness and snarled at me.

"I want you to die."

He was dying. I could see it behind all that rage. My magic was slithering through him, wrapping around his essence. I'd done this before with vampires; it empowered them, invigorated them. Apparently, my magic did not have the same influence on the living. Oops.

I could take it back. I knew that I could. I'd done that too. It wouldn't be all that different from twining a ball of string, but I certainly couldn't do it while he was suffocating me.

"Just die! I need you to die!"

"Well, that's just too bad," I said as he struggled to wrap his hands tighter around my throat. "I don't feel like dying."

I bucked my hips up, dislodging him from me. Had he been heavier, it wouldn't have worked, but in my dreamscape, he didn't weigh anything at all. I slammed my hand into his throat, and sent the other into his face. It was fast and vicious.

"I...I can...take it back," I coughed as he rolled back.

"Liar!"

I could. I wasn't lying. I reached my hand out to try, to prove it, but he threw up that invisible bubble of protection again, shielding himself behind his own power. It wasn't as strong. He was dying, and it showed in his magic.

"Stay back, witch!"

So much hate. I could understand him being upset. I had inadvertently hurt him, but I could also heal him, or at least take back what I had done. Sure, he was my enemy, and he had completely different views on the way magic ought to be practiced, but this slow and steady corruption wasn't really a cool way to go. But it was clear that he didn't want my hands anywhere near him. He didn't want my help.

"I can help you!"

"You will destroy the world!"

I didn't roll my eyes, but I really wanted to. "Are you serious? Do you really believe that? I have no intention of destroying anything."

"You didn't intend this either," he said, stretching his hands out and showing off his desiccated body, "but look what your magic has wrought."

He looked even worse. Maybe it was the moment or all the effort he had put into hurting me, but he looked like a thousand-year-old man with paper thin skin and no hair. He was crumbling right in front of me as a phantom wind swept around us.

"No," I shook my head, "I didn't do this. This happened because you decided to keep me locked up in your damn compound. If you had approached me like a human being, like a person, and told me what you thought about this whole prophecy business, I would have listened with open ears. But no. My mom snatched me up with magic, and you guys locked me in a room while you were literally draining the life from an innocent vampire."

His lips, peeling like cheap wallpaper, broke and bled as he smiled. Trails of red outlined his teeth. "Innocent? You think he is innocent?"

I sighed. "If this is the part where you tell me that he can't be trusted, you are a little too late. I've figured it out myself."

I wasn't being entirely honest, but it was close. Besides, it was totally worth the little lie to see that gross grin wiped off of his face. Then, it all twisted up again, and he shot his magic at me. I was ready for it. The shield that I'd been picturing over and over during this dream shot to my arm, and I used it to block the magic.

"Stop this. I can help you."

"No!" he snarled, his voice as brittle as leaves in a forest fire. "You'll kill me."

"I don't want to."

"Liar!"

I sighed. "I won't hurt myself to prove you wrong; stop this. Stop this now!"

He didn't. He threw raw magic at me over and over again. But he was weak, and weakening with every motion. I knew that he didn't have long. I wanted to help him; really, I did. I didn't like the idea of me being the reason anyone died, but I also wasn't going to sacrifice myself for his temporary comfort.

"Die!" he snarled.

I peeked out over the top of my shield. His skin was peeling away from his body. He was a wreckage of his former glory. That wasn't good. His hands were in front of him, the long, aged fingers forming a sphere. I could feel the collection of magic building there. He was putting the last of himself into this attack, and I didn't think I was going to survive it. No, I realized, I knew that I wasn't going to make it.

I reached out with my own magic, finding those tendrils of necromancy swimming through him. I tugged at them; I could have pulled them back. I could have saved him, but I knew that he wouldn't let me survive even if I did. Instead of pulling them back, I fed them.

He screamed. His body jerked, and all that magic he had been building exploded around him like a bomb. Flashes of memories that weren't mine skipped across the gray nothingness, and, for just a moment, I knew him a little better.

Instead of musing over them, I jerked awake and took what felt like my first breath in far too long.

The face that looked at me bore little similarity to my own, but it was familiar.

"Dad?" I asked.

His eyes were filled with concern. "Lore? Are you alright?"

I had to think about that. I tried to lift my arms, but they felt heavy. "I... don't know."

"You've been asleep for a long time."

I wasn't sure I wanted to know the answer to my next question. "How long?"

He looked over his shoulder. I turned my head to follow the line of his gaze. Jenny and Reikah were sitting together on the couch that I could just barely see from my position on the bed. It was dark, very dark.

"A week."

"Are you serious?" I asked, struggling to sit up. It hurt. No, it didn't. I didn't feel any pain, just a great heavy weight keeping me down. "What happened? What are you doing here? Where is Wei?"

He placed a hand on my hand. I was grateful that I could actually feel it. "You were trapped in that dreamscape, but you needed to be. We took turns keeping you asleep."

I felt a twinge of anger. "Okay. What about the rest of it?"

"I came back because you needed me."

I hadn't expected that. I couldn't remember the last time that my dad had really done anything for me. He had moved me around a lot, sure, with my safety in mind, but that wasn't for me. That was because he was afraid, so really it had been for him. If he'd done all of that for me, he would have told me the truth from the beginning and let me decide what to do.

"Oh," I said dumbly.

"I'm sorry if you aren't' feeling well. It's been a long time since I used my magic."

Oh right. My father was a witch. I had forgotten. It wasn't easy for me to reconcile the everyday businessman vision that I had of my father and the idea of a magical spellcaster.

"I didn't know you could heal," I said. "That's what you did, right? In the dream?"

He nodded slowly, looking pretty tired. "It is. You were hurt. I did what I could."

"You helped," I promised. "Thank you."

We shared a long, awkward silence. My father and I, despite having only one another for a lot of my childhood, weren't what I would call close. Maybe I had always known that he was keeping something from me, or maybe I just hated him for making us go from one place to the other with no other explanation but work.

I looked out the window. A week had completely changed the world outside. It was snowing, and had been for quite some time. Piles of it hid the road and even the small patch of lawn in front of my grandmother's house. No, I corrected myself for the zillionth time, it was my house. I had earned it. I had nearly died, not once but twice. The first time had been at the Order of the Loyal Hermit's compound; the second had been within my own dreams. I had cleaned it out, even taken up some of the shelves with my stuff. This was my place, and I couldn't keep thinking of it as belonging to my grandmother.

"I'm sorry, Lorena."

I looked back at him. The moonlight was reflecting off the snow bright enough to illuminate the entire room. For as long as I had known him, my father had always dressed in the uniform of mid-level business: khakis, button-down shirts, and loafers. Tonight, though, he wore a loose-fitting t-shirt and jeans. It was a little jarring. His hair, a few shades darker than my own ash brown, with a few strands of silver woven artistically through it, had grown to his shoulders rather than its normal ear length. He looked like my dad, but not all at the same time.

"I was wrong," he continued, "I should have told you about the prophecy. I should have given you a choice. I could tell you that I was just being a protective father, but for the life of me, I can't think of a time when that's been a good excuse for anything a dad has done for his kid."

I wasn't going to argue, but even if I wanted to, I was shocked to silence.

"When I was a kid," he said, "I got made fun of. Everyone on the mountain knew who my mother was and what she could do. Quinn witches were a bit of a local legend. When I was young, I thought it was cool. Here my mom was, a woman who could just make things happen, who saw things before they happened, and my father was stupidly in love with her. Then, I went to school, and it all changed. I showed off a little, and it scared some people and bothered the rest."

He stood up and walked around the bed, adjusting the curtains over the screen. My father had a terrible habit of fidgeting when he was nervous about something. I remember him doing similar things every time he was about to tell me that we were moving.

"I'm sorry," I said.

He shook his head. "It's just an excuse at the end of the day, Lorena. I could probably have had the greatest experience, and I may have made the exact same decision. When I heard what my mother had to say, I was...I was in a poor state of mind."

"My mother," I said softly.

He nodded. "You've met her then."

"I wasn't give much of a choice. She has...a way with manipulation."

He laughed, but it wasn't a happy laugh. It was the very definition of bitter. "She does. I'm sorry I never told you about her."

"I can't imagine it would have been a happy conversation to have."

He shook his head. "But parents don't get to choose to just have comfortable conversations with their children. That was my fault. I'm going to help you, whatever you want to do."

It was so weird. Here my dad was telling me everything that I had ever wanted to hear. There was a terrified part of me that wondered if this wasn't just some other dream, that I wasn't trapped. I looked down at my arms, seeing the smeared sigils there that would have kept me in lucid dreams. I could see bruises, ugly and yellow in all the places that I had been hurt, and there, at my feet, was Maahes.

"Thanks," I said, continuing to be the universal master of the awkward conversation. "Right now, I just want to know where Wei is."

He gave me a look, and I felt my guts twist into knots.

"They've found him, right? It's been a week," I whispered it, really hoping that the terrible thought in my head was wrong.

"We know where he is, Lorena, but he's dead."

Well, I thought to myself, I guess I wasn't dreaming.

To Be Concluded....

***

Ready for the final part of the story?

Dear Reader,

I want to personally thank you for taking your time to read "***House Of Vampires II***" I really hope you enjoyed it and you are hungry for the next part in the story.

"House Of Vampires 3" is available to pre-order now and if you do so you get it for 99c instead of $2.99 so if you want to it delivered to your device on release date then follow the link below and pre-order right away!

PRE-ORDER HOUSE OF VAMPIRES 3

See you in the next book :)

  Samantha x x

Get Yourself a FREE Bestselling Paranormal Romance Book!

Join the "**Simply Shifters**" Mailing list today and gain access to an exclusive **FREE** classic Paranormal Shifter Romance book by one of our bestselling authors along with many others more to come. You will also be kept up to date on the best book deals in the future on the hottest new Paranormal Romances. We are the HOME of Paranormal Romance after all!

* Get FREE Shifter Romance Books For Your Kindle & Other Cool giveaways

* Discover Exclusive Deals & Discounts Before Anyone Else!

* Be The FIRST To Know about Hot New Releases From Your Favorite Authors

Click The Link Below To Access Get All This Now!

SimplyShifters.com

**Already subscribed?
OK,** *Turn The Page!*

ALSO BY SIMPLY SHIFTERS....

SIMPLY VAMPIRES
A TEN BOOK VAMPIRE ROMANCE COLLECTION

99c or FREE to read with Kindle Unlimited

This unique 10 book package features some of the best selling authors from the world of Paranormal Romance. The perfect blend of love, sex and adventure involving curvy, cute heroines and their handsome vampire lovers.

Book 1 - JJ Jones – The White Vampire
Book 2 – Samantha Snow – A Lighter Shade Of Pale
Book 3 - Amira Rain – Melted By The Vampire
Book 4 - Serena Rose – Prince Lucien
Book 5 – Ellie Valentina – Red Solstice
Book 6 - Bonnie Burrows – The Vampire's Shared Bride
Book 7 - Jade White – Never Have A Vampires Baby
Book 8 – Angela Foxxe – A Billion Secrets
Book 9 - Samantha Snow - Spawn Of The Vampire
Book 10 - Jasmine White – Bitten By The Bad Boy

TAP HERE TO DOWNLOAD THIS NOW!

Printed in Great Britain
by Amazon